CHAPTER I

DARK DEEDS

"Good morning, Bigglesworth. Come in. Take a pew. help yourself to cigarettes." Air Commodore Raymond, head of the special Air Section at Scotland yard, pushed the cigarette-box within easy reach of his chief operational pilot.

Biggles took a cigarette and flicked his lighter, glancing sideways at his chief with humour making little wrinkles round the corners of his eyes. "I have a feeling that such cheerful generosity so early in the morning is to prepare me for something more sinister than cigarettes."

"Quite right," acknowledged the Air Commodore. "As usual, I'm having a spot of bother."

"Where is the shoe pinching this time?"

"Africa."

"North, south, east or west?"

"I don't know."

"There's a lot of difference."

"So I believe." The Air Commodore smiled lugubriously. "Your best plan, I think, would be to start somewhere about the middle of the continent."

"And what am I to look for?"

"A black man."

"As there are quite a number of black men in Africa that shouldn't be difficult."

"I have a particular one in view."

"Ah! I was afraid of that. Is there something peculiar about him?"

"There are several peculiar things about him and none of them is nice. He stands six foot six and is broad in proportion. That should help you to recognise him."

"This heavyweight has, I take it, been making a nuisance of himself?"

"He has, and he still is. Nuisance is hardly the right word, though. He's a menace, and, as things are going, an extremely dangerous one. Take it easy for a minute while I tell you about him—or as much as is known, which is little enough."

"I'm listening," stated Biggles.

The Air Commodore settled back in his chair. "The story begins roughly three years ago, when a name became the subject of native whispers. It was Cetezulu. It belonged, so rumour asserted, to a gigantic native who had dubbed himself with the somewhat ambitious title of the Black Elephant. The gentleman has now gone a little further. Today he styles himself the Black Elephant, Lord of Africa. Don't smile. There's nothing funny about it. The elephant part of the name was not ill-chosen. As you probably know, bull elephants have a habit of turning rogue. No rogue elephant has done as much mischief as this one. Rogue elephants are notoriously cunning. The rogue with which we are concerned is as elusive as if he were inspired by the devil himself.

"At home, in the first place, we didn't take this gentleman seriously. Neither did the people on the spot, if it comes to that. But they do now. So do we. For this scoundrel has embarked upon a career of wholesale murder and robbery without parallel anywhere in the last fifty years—and that's saying something. I will enlarge upon that in a moment. His avowed intention, as his adopted name implies, is to make himself master of Africa. In that respect he may be genuine. Dictatorship has become a sort of epidemic. The world is full of people who think they were born to run, first their own country, then the continent, and ultimately, no doubt, the universe. Here we have a black man bitten by this bug. Notice the name—Cetezulu. It is obviously an assumed one, embodying the name of two of Africa's most famous black warriors: Cetewayo and Dinizulu. It is said that Cetezulu claims descent from Charca, the great Zulu king. Certain it is that he affects the old Zulu warrior's equipment—leopard-skin, ostrich feathers and so on. The few

6

Biggles and the Black Raider

Captain W. E. Johns

First published in the U.K. by
Hodder & Stoughton Ltd., London,
This edition was first published in Armada in 1970 by
Fontana Paperbacks
14 St. James's Place, London SW1A 1PF.

This impression 1978.

Printed in Great Britain by
Love & Malcomson Ltd., Brighton Road,
Redhill, Surrey.

who have seen this fellow and survived are agreed that he is a spectacular figure of a man."

"Where did he come from in the first place?" enquired Biggles.

"There are plenty of opinions about that; but the truth is, nobody knows for certain," answered the Air Commodore. "One story is that he was born in Kimberley and at one time worked in the mines there; but having killed a foreman, he bolted. Others say that he came from as far north as the Sudan. Some believe he was born in Kenya and was brought up at a Mission School there. But as I say, nobody knows for certain, although from the fact that he speaks English well we may assume that he was once in contact with white men." The Air Commodore smiled wryly. "Maybe, it was from them that he got the dictator idea, if he is genuine in that. He may not be. That may be merely a cover for his villainy, to impress the credulous natives. But let us stick to what we know." The Air Commodore reached for a cigarette.

He resumed. "What we might call the first official appearance of this trouble-maker was in a native Reserve in Kenya, where he became conspicuous as an agitator determined to stir up strife with the workers. He overdid it when, having got into debt at the store, he hit the store-keeper on the head with a bottle and departed before the police could lay their hands on him. He was next heard of as a game poacher—and some of the native methods of trapping wild animals were not pretty. The game ranger who went after him was murdered out of hand. From that time he has moved about Africa, leaving a trail of the most brutal murders. He has killed blacks and whites without discrimination, seizing their possessions and burning their homes. In a word, he has instigated a reign of terror which, if it goes on, will end in much of the country being depopulated. People are leaving their homes and going to the cities for protection. When I say he moves about Africa, I mean that literally. He strikes here, there and everywhere. Today he might be in Northern Rhodesia. In a week we may hear of him in Uganda. Within a fortnight he may be in the French or Belgian Congos, or Portuguese Angola."

"How does he manage that?"

The Air Commodore stubbed his cigarette. "It seems that he has developed the same technique as his namesake, the elephant. There are still a good many wild herds in Africa. While they behave themselves they are reasonably safe. Indeed, they are protected by law. But there are some bad hats among them who have tried to make a living the easy way by making night raids on the natives' mealie patches and banana plantations. The natives complain, not without reason, whereupon a white hunter goes out to administer punishment calculated to discourage this practice. In fact, some of the older animals are shot. The others know why. Unfortunately, they are not necessarily cured of their bad habits and several lessons may be necessary. In the end, it becomes a game of tip-and-run. A herd, knowing that punishment will follow a raid, puts as great a distance as possible between itself and the inevitable pursuit.

"These are the tactics employed by Cetezulu. He strikes, and runs, travelling only by night and hiding in thick cover by day. Which means, really, that he disappears. He moves far and fast. We have it on record that he has travelled fifty miles a day for a week. Imagine what that means. It's practically impossible to catch up with him. It may be a week, or even a month, before word of his latest crime reaches the authorities. In that time he may have moved hundreds of miles in any direction. With millions of square miles in which to operate it has so far been impossible to get near him. He is rarely seen, with the result that everybody, black and white, is on the jump, wondering if he is next on the list."

"I imagine he isn't running this racket single-handed?"

"Oh dear no. He started in a small way, but success has enlarged his gang until, so it is said, it numbers thirty or more. Dictators are never short of supporters to share in the loot. Men like Cetezulu attract to themselves others of their own kidney and therein lies the greatest danger.

8

Unless something is soon done to end the career of this scoundrel we may expect his gang to grow to hundreds, and eventually, perhaps thousands. It is said that he is forcing men to join him—black men, of course, holding out the promise of a black African empire for the Africans. Some tribes that have refused to co-operate with him have had their villages burnt and their cattle stolen. Natives live on their cattle. To lose them means starvation. One can hardly blame them, therefore, if they choose to serve the Black Elephant rather than invite certain death."

"But surely some of the law-respecting tribes are strong enough to resist this rascal?"

"One would think so, but so far that has not been the case. The trouble is, the very name, Black Elephant, has become something to strike terror. Anyway, the fact remains that when the whisper goes round that the Black Elephant is approaching, people either fly for their lives or put at his disposal everything they possess."

"You don't mean that the white settlers do that?"

"What else can a man do but get out of the way, particularly if he has a wife and family? At first, not realising the desperate nature of the danger, most of them faced it, and lost their lives. They realise now that there is nothing they can do. All ranches, coffee estates and the like, depend entirely on native labour. Mention of the Black Elephant is enough to scatter them. The white proprietor or manager is left alone. Even though he has weapons, and he usually has guns and rifles, what hope has he of holding off an attack by thirty or more black fanatics? His only chance is to get wind of the impending raid and bolt. In that case he may save his life, but only at the cost of everything else he possesses. He returns to find his house razed, his cattle gone and his crops destroyed. Up to date the Black Elephant has murdered not fewer than twenty whites and an unknown number of black people. He has killed hundreds of Indian traders and labourers. He seems to hate them."

"And this, you say, has been going on for three years?"

"Yes, but it has got rapidly worse during the last few months."

"It's time it was stopped."

"It will have to be stopped, before more blacks join this villain or follow his example. The trouble is not confined to us. Every country with possessions in Africa comes into this ugly picture."

"What has been done about it so far?"

"Plenty. But nothing has been achieved. Apart from the fact that to locate this man is about as hopeful a proposition as looking for a flea in a flock of sheep, ordinary ground forces are too slow, even though they are provided with motor transport. Cars, jeeps, motor-cycles and light vans, can only operate on tracks or smooth ground. Cetezulu knows that perfectly well and stays in rough country, which is not difficult in Africa. As I told you at the beginning, this black devil moves across country at fantastic speed. The last raid, two days ago, was a particularly horrible murder in Northern Rhodesia. A white woman and her four children, with one or two loyal black servants, were burnt alive in their own bungalow. The husband had gone to Broken Hill on business. The Black Elephant had apparently been hiding just inside the Belgian Congo. There is no indication of which way the murderers have gone. They may have gone north to Uganda, east to Mozambique or west to Angola. You see how hopeless it is. Police, game rangers, and the Askaris, have all been out, but it is like chasing a will-o'-the-wisp."

"How many people have actually seen this brute?"

"Few have seen him at close quarters and survived. The best witness we have, a very lucky fellow, is a Masai tribesman named Mishu. He was gun-bearer to Major Harvey, a game warden, whom he saw murdered. That was about three months ago. Harvey claimed that Mishu was the steadiest gun-bearer in Africa. They had worked together for years."

"What happened?"

"Well, it seems that a travelling missionary brought in a tale about a man-eating leopard. Harvey went to in-

10

vestigate but he didn't find it. While he was in the district he shot an old bull buffalo that had killed several natives in the Mapika district. The beast did not drop to his shot but blundered off into an area of elephant-grass and bamboo. Harvey dared not leave it there in that condition, of course, because it would have been a bigger danger than ever. So with Mishu he took a chance and followed it into cover. Instead of finding the buffalo, they found themselves suddenly face to face with Cetezulu and his gang. They had evidently spent the night there. Harvey may not have realised who the men were. Anyway, before he could speak, Cetezulu had flung an assegai which killed him on the spot. Mishu would have been next, no doubt, but at that moment the wounded buffalo, which must have circled round on its tracks as they sometimes do, arrived on the scene, steaming for revenge. There was a stampede, and in the general panic Mishu managed to hide in the bamboo until it got dark, when Cetezulu cleared off. Mishu had a good view of him. He describes him as an enormous man, with a slight cast in one eye, dressed in full Zulu chief regalia. A punitive force of police was rushed to the spot, but the Black Elephant had done his usual vanishing trick. He next popped up in Tanganyika, where he burned a native village after looting the local store."

Biggles tapped the ash off his cigarette with thoughtful care. "Why are you telling me about this?"

"I thought you might be able to make a suggestion as to how we could get to grips with this fiend."

"You're not going to suggest, I hope, that my total strength of four men is capable of arresting thirty or more black desperadoes—even if we could find them?"

"Er—no."

"What can I do about it then?"

"That's what I want you to tell me."

Biggles thought for a moment. "You say that when Cetezulu raids a ranch, he makes off with the cattle?"

"Yes. In Africa cattle are money."

"You can put money in a bank, but cattle take up more

11

room. What does he do with the stolen property?"

"How would I know? Does it matter?"

"It might. I take it he has raided several ranches?"

"Yes. He must have taken hundreds of head of cattle."

"More than he could eat?"

"Good gracious! Yes."

"Then I repeat, what does he do with them?"

"Why do you ask?"

"Because if he hasn't eaten this stock, he must have put it somewhere for safe-keeping, until such time as he can find a market for it, even if he has a market for it now; in Abyssinia, for instance, where there is always a market for cattle. The stuff must still be on the hoof. He's bound to have a hide-out somewhere, where there is an ample water supply for the herd. To that place he is also bound to return at intervals, to make sure that the stuff is all right."

"That's true."

"Then instead of looking for this elusive brigand, I suggest it might be more profitable to look for the stolen cattle, which will be less mobile than he is."

"And then?"

"That's where you should catch him. Instead of chasing wild geese, it's better to wait for them to come to you."

"First of all you've got to find this hide-out. That would be difficult."

"Granted. But I submit that it's easier than looking for something that's always on the move. You asked me for a suggestion. That's it. If you can think of something better, go ahead."

"In an aircraft you could cover a lot of ground," conceded the Air Commodore.

"That's what I was thinking," answered Biggles. "As much ground could be searched in a week as would take a ground force a year. Moreover, we should be on a look-out from an angle for which the Lord of Africa might not have made allowances. It would be a comparatively easy matter to construct a stockade that might be passed

12

unnoticed from ground level; but it would not be so easy
to roof it over so that it couldn't be spotted from above."

"I think you've got something there," agreed the Air
Commodore. "I see one big snag. Native herds of cattle
are dotted about the whole of Africa. How will you know
which is the right one?"

"By trial and error. One would have a guide, anyway."

"What sort of guide?"

"Water. Cattle, whether they are standing still or on
the move, need water all the time. No matter how far
away from the scenes of his crimes the Black Elephant's
cattle compound may be, of one thing you may be sure.
There will be, along the route, a series of lakes, or rivers,
waterholes or what have you, within a day's march of
each other. Cetezulu, not being a fool, would take that
into account when selecting his line of retreat. There are
big areas of Africa where water does not occur at all.
They can be ruled out. Follow your chain of water-holes
and at the end of one of them you'll find the stolen cattle.
Wait by the cattle and sooner or later the Lord of Africa
will roll up to count his wealth."

"Would you like to take on the job?"

Biggles sighed. "I was afraid it would come to that."

The Air Commodore smiled. "You knew it would,
from the start of the discussion. Already you've provided
a clue which no one else seems to have thought of. Will
you go?"

"What exactly do you want me to do?"

"Arrest this self-appointed Lord of Africa, of course."

Biggles shook his head. "Nothing doing. I've too much
regard for my body to offer it as a pin-cushion for asse-
gais. This man and his gang are murderers. They know
that if they're caught they'll swing. They'll see to it that
they don't get caught. Not fewer than fifty men would be
needed to fight it out with that bunch of savages."

"If he attempted to use force you would be justified in
doing the same thing."

"In other words, I wait until I have a spear stuck in me
and then I can shoot back. Oh no. There's only one

sensible way of dealing with an armed murderer—shoot first."

"That's a bit savage."

"We're dealing with a savage. Kid glove methods will get you nowhere except in a wooden box under the ground. I'm not suggesting shooting the fellow in the back, or when he's asleep, or anything like that. I'd employ the methods we used in the R.A.F. with certain tribes on the North-West Frontier and the Middle East. You remember the procedure. First you dropped leaflets inviting them to give themselves up for a fair trial. If that doesn't work, you make a demonstration by flying over them to let them see you mean business. That's a fair enough warning. If it doesn't have the desired effect— well, you give them a taste of musket balls. In other words, if they prefer it that way, that's how they can have it. The choice is theirs. Of course, if, having found the man, one was in radio contact with a highly mobile ground force, one could call them up and leave the business to them. It would mean moving fast. One night would be enough for the Black Elephant to slip away out of reach—from what you tell me."

"I'd be content to leave everything to your discretion," announced the Air Commodore. "The thing is to get this devil buttoned up before he can kill anyone else. If he goes on as he is, he may soon have a small army behind him, and that would be a more serious matter still."

"All right; as long as we're clear about that," agreed Biggles. "It's the only sensible way. Don't expect me to invite suicide by employing lily-fingered tactics with a mass murderer. This Black Elephant reckons on brutality for success. We'll see how that lines up against modern methods. I'll take on the job on the understanding that there's no interference by bureaucrats at home. I want no bleating in the House of Commons about a poor innocent native being shot. I'll have my orders in writing, too. I'm not being made a scapegoat for a political racket."

The Air Commodore smiled at Biggles's vehemence.

14

"All right. You get this black devil and you can rely on me to back you up if anyone lets out so much as a squeak."

"Fair enough. I take on this job knowing that the Black Elephant will kill me if he can. Others have tried to do that. If they get hurt themselves in the process I don't saturate my pillow with tears worrying about it. In this case, if one of us has to get shot, I shall do my best to see that it isn't me. As long as we're clear about that, I'll go ahead."

"Very well. Let me know how I can help you."

"There's one thing I'd like to examine while I'm getting ready, and that's the complete list of outrages thought to have been committed by the Black Elephant. If, as I imagine, he's covering the ground he knows best, it may give me a line to work on."

The Air Commodore agreed. "I'll send you up the complete report right away."

Biggles rose. "Thanks. I'll go and get my maps out."

CHAPTER 2

PLANS AND PREPARATIONS

TEN days after his conversation with the Air Commodore, Biggles and his team were at Kampala, the largest township in Uganda, in Central Africa, on the northern littoral of Lake Victoria, where a furnished bungalow conveniently near the airport had been put at the disposal of Scotland Yard by British Overseas Airways. A native cook, an elderly negress named Lulu, had been "laid on" by the same company to attend to the kitchen arrangements.

Not knowing how long he would be in Africa Biggles had decided that it was essential that they should base themselves somewhere on the main trunk route down the continent where communications, maintenance, stores and radio, as well as servicing facilities, were available for the three machines which he had selected as best suited for the work on hand. These were a Mosquito with full war armament, on loan from the R.A.F., a Proctor and an Auster. All were fitted with long range tanks and high-frequency radio telephony. A considerable amount of equipment, which need not be detailed but which covered everything Biggles thought he was likely to require, had been carried out by one of the big machines of the B.O.A.C. regular service. The aircraft, on account of their different speeds, had been flown out independently. Biggles, with Ginger as second pilot, had flown straight on in the Mosquito to make preparations for what might turn out to be a long stay at the bungalow. Algy and Bertie, following in their own time, had arrived three days later.

Kampala had been chosen as the most central spot from which to operate. To the north lay the Sudan, Ethiopia, and the most easterly point of French Equatorial Africa. To the west spread the vast territory of the Belgian Congo. To the east Kenya. To the south were Northern Rhodesia and Nyasaland. There had been rumours of Cetezulu being in all these countries. Kampala was, therefore, more or less in the middle of the area being threatened by him. Even so, the distances that might have to be covered were such that Ginger, on the way down, was appalled by the magnitude of the task they had undertaken. The half-million square miles in which the Black Elephant had been known to operate comprised every imaginable sort of country, from sea level to plateaus rising many thousands of feet, wherein were to be found plains, swamps, mountains, deserts, jungles and tropical forests, all on a gigantic scale. In a moment of pessimism he voiced to Biggles his doubts about the outcome of the expedition.

"I'll give you a tip worth remembering," answered Biggles sagely. "It was given to me by a Nepalese who spent most of his life hauling loads on his back up the Himalayas. He said it was a mistake to look too far ahead. He admitted that if he looked too often at the top of the mountain up which he had to climb, he would either sit down or go back. The size of the job would knock the heart out of him. So he never looked up. He only looked down—and kept on plodding. It was easier that way. Get the idea? You can apply that method to any stiff undertaking, such as the one we're on now."

Ginger agreed that there might be something in it.

How the marauders were to be dealt with even if they were located had been more or less left in the air for the simple reason that the situation, and the method of handling it, would depend largely on where contact was made. In a rather vague sort of way it had been suggested that the best course would be for Biggles to call up either police or native troops, or both, on the radio, and leave the ground forces to make the arrests. It was realised that this might be easier in theory than in practice. Military forces were few and far between, and even though they possessed light trucks and other mechanical transport it would probably take them days, or even weeks, to reach the objective, only to find that the raiders were no longer there. Trucks would be useless in rough country, anyway; and if it came to foot slogging it was unlikely that a disciplined body of men, carrying the equipment they would require, would be able to overtake the lightly-clad raiders, who could be kept under observation from the air by day but not by night. The method of dealing with them had therefore been left to Biggles's discretion. Anyhow, as he remarked, the first thing was to find them.

Nothing fresh had transpired since Biggles had accepted the assignment, although a study of the long list of outrages had produced a sort of pattern that provided for speculation. From the dates and locations of the raids, it seemed—as Biggles pointed out to the others—that the Black Elephant worked in a definite cycle, travelling

17

in a great circle and striking at intervals. But—and this was the point—it was always following a raid far to the north that a lull occurred, as if the raiders were taking a rest from their considerable exertions.

While admitting that the gang would have to rest somewhere, sometime, Biggles claimed that this itinerary supported his view that Cetezulu had a hide-out for the accumulation of his loot. If the regular lull that followed a northern raid meant that the gang were resting, it followed that the hiding-place lay in that direction. It was, Biggles conceded, a slender clue considering the size of the country involved; but they had to start somewhere.

Bertie had an opinion on this aspect, based on his experience of foxes and fox-hunting. The fox, he said, was by general consent the most cunning of all animals, although some of the big game animals in Africa, after being hunted constantly, could run him pretty close. Cetezulu might be expected to employ the same sort of cunning. The fox did not kill on his own doorstep, thus betraying the whereabouts of his lair. He went far afield to make a kill. The place to look for him, therefore, was where his usual prey remained undisturbed, where there were no signs of him. Following this line of argument, the place to look for the Black Elephant's retreat was in a district where there had never been a raid.

Biggles admitted that there might be something in this and said he would bear it in mind, particularly as such an area occurred in the extreme north. An argument against this theory was, the Black Elephant would probably do most of his raiding in the south in any case, because the most valuable loot was to be found there. There was little in the north—merely native kraals and an occasional trader or prospector. Still, the Black Elephant had certainly been in the north, because one of his murders, that of Major Harvey, the game warden, had occurred near the Bunyoro Reserve, in Uganda.

Algy asked, if Cetezulu did not normally kill in the locality of his hide-out, why had he revealed his position by killing the game warden, for all he could have got out of that was the dead man's rifle, and stores that had presumably been abandoned?

Biggles answered that Cetezulu had probably killed Harvey for the very reason that the game warden had by accident discovered him, so his whereabouts would have been reported in any case. By killing Harvey, Biggles asserted, Cetezulu had hoped to avoid the very thing he had succeeded in doing, which was to call attention to his position. This was due to the fortuitous arrival on the scene of the wounded buffalo, which had enabled Mishu the gun-bearer to escape and report the matter at Administrative Headquarters.

Actually, further light was thrown on this when Mishu was fetched from Nairobi by Algy in the Proctor. Mishu came willingly, and not only gave his version of the affair, but threw some interesting sidelights on the whole business.

He turned out to be a middle-aged man typical of the warlike Masai tribe to which he belonged—tall, sinewy, thin-lipped, proud, and somewhat taciturn. He had not, Ginger was pleased to note, adopted the semi-European style of dress affected by many natives, but still wore the simple loin-cloth with a few ornaments. His chest and arms bore the scars of more than one encounter with wild animals. There was nothing unusual about this, since in order to qualify for manhood a Masai must kill a lion with his spear. As a matter of detail, Biggles knew from reading some of Major Harvey's reports that Mishu had won a reputation even among his own people as a lion-killer, for which reason he had been taken on as a gun-bearer, a job that calls for the highest courage, nerve and coolness, since in facing up to a charge by lion, buffalo or elephant, the gun-bearer puts his life in the hands of his master, who does the shooting.

From his long employment by white hunters Mishu spoke English fairly well, although in a high-pitched, sing-song drawl that fascinated Ginger until he became accustomed to it. His manner was serious and reserved.

Apart from being able to describe the general appearance of the Black Elephant he had little information that was not already in Biggles's possession. He confirmed that Cetezulu was an exceptionally big man whose height was exaggerated by an ostrich feather headdress. If the man carried firearms, Mishu said he did not see them. At the time of their brief encounter he had noticed only a broad-bladed assegai and the almond-shaped Zulu shield of ox-hide. Mishu had certain opinions, however, to which Biggles paid close attention.

He said he believed the Black Elephant to be a man who, some years back, had caused a lot of trouble as a game poacher in the Semliki and Guru Reserves. To what tribe this man belonged he did not know, but he was certainly not a Zulu. He and Major Harvey had often looked for this poacher but had only once caught a glimpse of him. He killed practically all the rhinos in the district, mostly by trapping, or poisoning, or other revolting practices. They always knew his work, when carcasses were found, by the way the horns were sawn off.

When Biggles expressed some surprise at this Mishu went on to explain that rhino horn had a considerable value in China where it was held in high esteem as a medicine. The horn, ground up, was worth thirty shillings or more a pound. There was reason to believe that the poacher sold his stuff to a trader from Ethiopia or Italian Somaliland. Mishu was convinced that the Black Elephant was the poacher of that time. He had merely widened the scope of his nefarious activities. At all events, he knew the same country intimately, and used the same tracks. The poacher knew that he was being sought by Major Harvey, who eventually hounded him out of the district. That was why, Mishu thought, Major Harvey had been murdered on sight. The Black Elephant recognised him and took his revenge.

"I see," said Biggles slowly. This revenge motive was of course a new development.

Mishu concluded by saying, quite calmly, that as he had lost his master, he himself was going to look for the Black Elephant, and kill him.

After a moment's reflection Biggles asked him, as they both had the same object in view, if he would care to join them. It was obvious that such a man would be useful in many ways.

Mishu did not jump at the offer: but he said yes, he would go with them. Perhaps they could help each other. So he became one of the party, making himself a bivouac in the garden of the bungalow and more or less keeping to himself except when his advice was sought, as it often was.

For the moment there was little that any of them could do except wait for a clue as to the Black Elephant's whereabouts. Nothing had been heard of him for some time, so to start anything like a serious search would be a haphazard proceeding that would only tire them, and put wear and tear on the machines to no purpose. It was better to stand by, Biggles decided, until they had something definite to work on. The airport radio would let them know if anything happened. Meanwhile, traders, game rangers, white hunters, and many native tribes were keeping watch for the would-be Black Emperor.

Biggles spent a good deal of time studying the pattern formed by the many outrages committed by the blood-thirsty negro. These he had marked on a map, which was pinned to a wall of the living-room. Sometimes he would call Mishu in for his opinion, and on more than one occasion this resulted in useful details coming to light. Maps, Mishu said, were in his opinion unreliable, in that they did not make allowances for the seasons. The chief lakes, rivers and water-holes, were always there, of course; but there were periods when, during the rains, water became available in districts where, according to the maps, there was only desert. For information about water, therefore, it was better to rely on local knowledge. This was of great interest to Biggles, who was still thinking on the lines of a water supply in connection with the movements of the stolen cattle.

It was Mishu, too, who introduced the further possibility that Biggles had not taken into account. Biggles

21

happened to remark that it was strange that the Black Elephant seemed to be able to move about unseen by native hunters, cow-herders and the like.

Mishu startled him by saying that it would be impossible for the Black Elephant to move about without being seen by such people. He was bound to be seen, and fairly often. If the Black Elephant himself was not seen, his tracks would certainly be seen, for the simple reason that it was impossible to move a large herd of cattle without leaving tracks. The cattle would have to be watered. Near water the ground is soft, and when the ground is soft it is impossible not to leave marks.

"Why, then, do people not report the presence of the Black Elephant when they see him?" demanded Biggles.

Mishu's explanation was simple. The Kaffirs—as he called Hottentots—were afraid to speak, for fear the Black Elephant would return and slay them. In their terror of him some native tribes, he did not doubt, would help him, and provide him and his followers with food if they were short. "You will remember, *bwana*," said Mishu simply, "this man tells everyone he will one day be king of Africa. They think this may be true. If he is one day king, then he will kill all people who did not help him to be king."

Biggles perceived that, from the natives' point of view, this was a sound argument. However, Mishu did not think that any of the natives who were comfortably settled in the reserves allotted to them would join the outlaws, unless they were forced to it by the threat of death. It was more likely, he thought, that Cetezulu's followers were men who had been in trouble in the big cities of the south. Such men were thieves by nature. But, of course, he added as an afterthought, if the Black Elephant became really powerful, then bad men from all over Africa might join him to make a big army.

Biggles became more and more glad that he had this shrewd Masai on hand to give him advice.

A week passed, and Ginger was beginning to get bored with doing nothing, when a runner arrived from the radio

22

room with a message. It was brief and to the point. The Black Elephant had struck again. The place was Ulunga, in Northern Rhodesia. A *safari* had been attacked and wiped out. A white hunter, two American sportsmen and some of their native porters, had been massacred. One wounded survivor had reached Kasama and reported the crime. It had taken him ten days.

"Let's get cracking," said Ginger crisply, after the message had been read aloud.

Biggles shook his head. "No use. There would be nothing to see when we got there. These murders took place ten days ago. By this time the Black Elephant will be hundreds of miles away." He turned to the map and marked a spot with a finger. "Here's Ulunga, at the foot of Lake Tanganyika. That's about eight hundred miles from here. While we were tearing down south Cetezulu would probably be heading north as fast as he could hook it. He wouldn't be likely to linger on the scene of his crime. That's if his previous record is anything to go by, and I see no reason why he should change his tactics. North Rhodesia seems to be about the southern limit of his operations. His next effort, I imagine, will be somewhere north of that, but in all probability still south of us. He should still be heading north. That means that he will travel up one side or the other of the lake, which, as you see, runs practically due north and south, a matter of four hundred and fifty miles. The question is, which side of the lake will he follow, the east bank or the west? Fortunately the lake is not very wide, between thirty and forty miles for the most part."

"D'you mean you're going to sit here and wait for this hound to kill somebody else?" cried Ginger in an astonished voice.

"I didn't say that," returned Biggles. "I said I could see no point in rushing eight hundred miles south while the man we're looking for is probably travelling north at full speed. We should do better, I think, to watch the shores of the lake. It's Belgian territory on the far side, but I don't think that matters much. The Belgians must be as sick of this scoundrel as we are. The only thing is, if Cetezulu sees too many planes flying up and down, not being a fool he may guess what they're looking for and take extra precautions against being seen."

"What do we look for, old boy, tell me that?" requested Bertie.

"The only thing we can look for is cattle on the move," answered Biggles. "That is, unless we can make contact with people on the Black Elephant's line of march. We might take some high-altitude photos from time to time to see if cattle appear in any of the pictures. There will usually be some cattle, of course, because most natives have cattle. I'm hoping to see a big herd on the move."

Mishu, who had been listening intently, and obviously following the conversation, stepped into the discussion. "I can help, *bwana*," he said. "Part of my tribe called the Illumbwa live on the Tanganyika side of the lake."

"You think they'll tell us if Cetezulu has gone through their territory?"

"No, *bwana*. No tell you. Tell me. I listen to talk, watch for tracks."

"If we took you there, would you do that?"

"Yes, *bwana*."

"What is the ground like where your people live?"

"Plenty flat plain with grass for cattle, same like this." Mishu indicated the nearby airfield with a sweep of his hand.

"Isn't there some risk of your people losing their cattle?"

"No. Cetezulu no touch. Masai too strong. Many good fighters."

"But I say, look here, old boy," put in Bertie speaking to Biggles. "Have you any proof that Cetezulu stays with his mob of cattle—if you see what I mean?"

"No, I haven't," admitted Biggles. "But I don't think he'll be far away. He can't dispose of the cattle anyway. I mean, he couldn't sell them. No one would have the actual cash to buy them. Or put it this way. In this part

24

of Africa wealth is reckoned in cattle. Isn't that right, Mishu?"

"Yes, *bwana*, that's right."

"I don't suppose for a moment that Cetezulu has with him all the cattle he has stolen on this particular expedition," went on Biggles. "There would be no sense in that. They would slow down his own movements and many would die from exhaustion on the way. No, that isn't the way it's done. It's a safe guess that to keep mobile he drops the cattle at intervals, where there is grazing, with a few herdsmen to look after them, and then collects them all on the way home—wherever that may be. The farther north he gets, therefore, the bigger the herd he's likely to have. What he does with them eventually is something we may one day discover." He turned back to Mishu. "Whereabouts along the lake do your people live?"

"They move sometimes for better grass, but never far from the north end," answered Mishu. He went on to explain that they did not all live together, but occupied several kraals spread over their Reserve, which covered a wide area. If Cetezulu headed north up the eastern side of Lake Tanganyika, he would have to pass through the Reserve.

"Assuming that Cetezulu is heading north, it's hardly likely that he would have reached there yet," surmised Biggles. "Four hundred odd miles in ten days would be fast going even for him, particularly if, as it is said, he travels mostly by night. What I suggest is, therefore, that you, Ginger, take Mishu in the Auster to the Illumbwa Reserve to keep watch while the rest of us take turns to make reconnaissance flights elsewhere."

"D'you want me to stay with Mishu?" asked Ginger.

"I think you'd better," replied Biggles. "There seems no point in leaving him there and burning a lot of petrol by dashing to and fro every day to see if he has any news. The place is a matter of about three hundred and fifty miles from here. Yes, you'd better stay. Then, if Cetezulu shows up, you could get word to me in an hour or two. If the Black Elephant is coming your way, he should be there pretty soon. If there is any delay I'll send Algy or Bertie to relieve you. You may see something of us in the other machines from time to time, anyway. Take some food with you. To be on the safe side, you'd better take some water, too."

"Where do I sleep?" enquired Ginger. "In the open with the lions or in one of Mishu's kraals?"

Biggles smiled and put the question to the Masai.

Mishu said it would be better to camp in the open. It was perfectly safe. If a white man was seen in one of the kraals, word would go round and people might wonder what he was doing. The Black Elephant might get to hear of it.

"That's your answer," Biggles told Ginger. "Take one of the small tents with you. All right, let's see about getting things fixed up. You've enough daylight left to make the trip today. The sooner you're down there the better."

CHAPTER 3

A CLOSE THING

LATER the same day found Ginger in the Auster, with Mishu, complete with assegai, sitting beside him, on a south-westerly course for Lake Tanganyika. As it is the longest lake in the world there was no possibility of missing it.

For the first two hundred miles, that other great inland sea, Lake Victoria, had formed the eastern horizon, while far to the west the fifteen thousand-foot peak of Mount Karisimbi cut into the sky like a colossal tooth to provide an unmistakable landmark. After another hour, a glittering streak across his bows told him that he was approaching the end of his journey; for which he was not sorry, for in the rarefied air, constant "bumps" tossed the machine about like a scrap of waste paper, making flying a matter of physical labour.

There was nothing of outstanding interest to be seen below. An occasional cluster of beehive-shaped huts with an overhanging smudge of smoke from the cooking fires; herds of native cattle, grazing; and, of course, a fair sprinkling of wild animals of the commoner sort, mostly wildebeest, zebra and giraffe. For the most part the terrain was more or less open, sometimes flat, sometimes undulating, with here and there low hills breaking into outcrops of rock at the top. Scrub and smallish trees, standing alone or in little groups, gave the landscape an untidy appearance. The prevailing colour was the greyish-brown of sun-scorched grass. In a word, it was typical African plateau scenery, and as such Ginger found it merely monotonous. After a while, there meandered across it a grey ribbon that was obviously a road of sorts. It followed the general direction of the lake, and gave Ginger his position, for it was marked on his map.

Mishu was apparently watching for it, for his manner became more alert and he surveyed the ground with renewed interest. After crossing the track, with the lake still about five miles distant, he made signs that it was time to go down.

Ginger throttled back, and while he was losing height made a close study of the area for the best landing-place. He expected no difficulty, for there were plenty of wide open spaces from which to choose and there was no wind to command any particular direction. However, he was taking no more chances than are inseparable from making a landing on an unknown surface, and he flew up and down several times at a low altitude to make sure there were no rocks, anthills, or other obstructions, likely to damage the machine. The rough, sun-dried grass did not appear to be long enough to pull the aircraft over on to its nose. Nor was it. The Auster came to a standstill in the brittle herbage which turned out to be about eighteen inches high, close to an open group of feathery-leaved mimosas into which he taxied, more with the object of taking advantage of the shade they provided than for any other reason. Satisfied with this position he switched off, jumped down and looked around. Not that there was much to look at except the cheerless landscape already described. It was still shining from the heat of the day although turning softly pink in the evening light. Apart from the mimosas, and one or two scrubby acacias, the only conspicuous feature was a fairly extensive patch of bushes mixed up with trees on some slightly higher ground about five hundred yards away. Not a soul was in sight nor could an animal of any sort be seen. It was, taking it by and large, Ginger thought, a depressing spot. Why Mishu had chosen it as their rendezvous he did not know, although he assumed there was some reason for it. It may have been the nearest flat patch to the people he wanted to see.

The aircraft was unloaded, and with the efficiency of long practice, Mishu made camp. The little tent was set up and a folding camp-bed erected in it. Food and water were put in handy positions, as was the rifle Ginger had brought with him. He did not expect to have to use it, but he derived a feeling of security from the fact that it was there. As soon as the camp was ship-shape, Mishu announced his intention of making enquiries, and without further parley set off in the direction of the setting sun, which also happened to be the direction of the lake. A broad fold in the ground hid the actual water from view.

Ginger watched him go, not without vague misgivings. This sort of thing was all very well for the Masai, who had been doing it all his life, he brooded. He wasn't exactly afraid of being left alone, for as far as he could see there was nothing to be afraid of; but like most people accustomed to living in a city he found there was something disconcerting in the fact that, although they were not to be seen, he was sharing the territory with some of the most dangerous animals in the world. Not to mention snakes, which he abhorred. In particular he had a wholesome respect for the black mamba, one of the few venomous snakes that had a reputation for attacking on

28

sight. He examined the ground around the camp closely for this highly efficient but unwelcome reptile.

His feeling of uneasiness did not diminish when the sun dropped behind the horizon, leaving a still, sultry darkness, in possession of the scene. He wished he had asked Mishu how long he thought he would be away. Mishu himself had not mentioned it. Perhaps he didn't know, pondered Ginger, who tried to comfort himself with the thought that more people are killed in cities by motor-cars than by the wild beasts of Africa. It was all a matter of familiarity. He understood the danger of taking chances with wheeled vehicles. Mishu understood the risks of colliding with lions, leopards and the like. An uneasy silence fell, so for something to do he lit a little fire, made a pot of coffee, and with his rifle handy had his supper of bread and corned beef. All remained quiet. The great African moon swung into the sky to touch everything with an eerie blue radiance. There was still no sign of Mishu.

Three hours later there was still no sign of him, so, realising that he could not sit up indefinitely, he retired to the tent, closed the flap, and without removing his clothes lay down in the hope of snatching some sleep—or at any rate, to get used to the sensation of trying to sleep with nothing between him and a possible maneater but a thin piece of canvas.

In this he failed dismally. Far from getting any sleep he became more and more awake. He found himself listening, although for what he did not know. He soon reached the stage of fancying that he could hear stealthy movements outside. He had just convinced himself that it was all imagination when the hush was shattered by a sound so horrible that his skin turned gooseflesh, as the expression is. The silly part of it was, he knew what had caused it. He had heard it before, more than once, for the mournful howl of the spotted hyena, once heard is never forgotten. It is one of the commonest night sounds in most parts of Africa; but that does not prevent it from being the most bloodcurdling noise in all nature. It begins

29

with a long drawn out moan, which rises until it ends in a wild shriek. This has been described as laughing. Ginger found it nothing to laugh at.

The beast was evidently hanging about the camp looking for food, in the choice of which the hyena is not in the least particular. Anything from old bones to new boots will do. Ginger did not remember leaving anything outside so he paid no further attention to the beast. Presently the animal was joined by a companion, and together they made the night so hideous with their grunts, gurgles and cackles, that Ginger soon had enough of it. The thought struck him that they might try their teeth on the tyres of the Auster. Muttering in his wrath he seized the first thing that he could lay his hands on, which happened to be a tin of condensed milk, and opened the flap. Seeing the beasts skulking ten yards away he flung the tin at them with a shout; whereupon they departed and did not return. He noticed that the fire had gone out, but he did not trouble to rekindle it.

He did not go back to bed at once, but stood gazing across the moonlit expanse, which was impossible not to admire. Standing there, presently a movement on the skyline caught his eye. Focusing on it, he made it out too be a native, walking quickly. Naturally, at first he took it to be Mishu, who, in returning, had got slightly off his course. But when he saw a second figure, then a third, and so on until there must have been more than a score, he knew that, whoever the men were, Mishu was not among them. A possible truth did not occur to him for a moment or two. He stood lost in a sort of wonder at the weird picture presented by the silent line of men as they stood sharply defined against the sky. They were, he noted, travelling from south to north.

That may have suggested their possible identity. The idea struck him like a blow, and sent him down on his hands and knees, although still watching. The Black Elephant! Could it be possible that he was seeing, on his first night out, the thing which he expected would take them weeks to find? At first it seemed too preposterous to be true. But then he saw that nothing could be more likely. It was not as though it was by accident that he was there. Biggles had stationed him on one of Cetezulu's most likely lines of march. The time factor was about right, too. The negro would just about have had time to reach the district. Biggles had worked the whole thing out from the evidence available, and it now looked as if his conclusions were correct.

The possibilities now presented threw Ginger into a curious state of mind that was a mixture of surprise, consternation and anxiety. He had found what he was looking for. What should he do about it? What *could* he do about it? He appeared to be in no immediate danger himself, for the men were several hundred yards away and moving on a course that would take them wide of his camp. He was not sure, but they seemed to be marching straight towards the area of bushes and trees that he had noted on landing. Was it their intention to halt there, he wondered. He watched closely, but his mental question was not answered. As the men neared the bushes they disappeared from sight, although whether this was because they had entered them, or marched straight on behind them, he could not tell. Once they were off the skyline it would not be possible to see them, anyway, he realised. They were too far away for that. For the same reason he would not hear any slight sounds they were likely to make.

For some little while Ginger stood there, his brain racing, torn by doubts and indecisions. There was nothing he could do single-handed. What he wanted, of course, was to let Biggles know as quickly as possible what he had seen. Just that and nothing more. But the only way that could be done was by flying back to Kampala. There were arguments against such a project at that moment. There would be danger in taking off in the dark over ground that he had not examined, for he could not be sure of taking off over the precise tracks he had made when landing. Cetezulu, if he was among the men he had seen, would hear the machine, and perhaps realise what it meant. Finally, there was Mishu. He could not very well leave him. So there he stood, nerves tingling, staring in the direction in which the men had disappeared. They had no cattle with them, he observed. But that meant nothing. They might have gone on ahead, or be following behind.

He decided that his best plan was to stay where he was, at any rate until daylight, when he would be able to see what he was doing. If Mishu returned, so well and good. If he did not, well, he would go back to Kampala anyway, report to Biggles, and then return for the Masai.

He had something else to think about when, with much thumping and snorting, a massive shape appeared, and moved towards him, from the direction he was watching. He soon saw that it was a rhinoceros. It had, fairly obviously, been disturbed by the natives he had seen. It came on, first at a trot, and then slowed down to a walk. Presently, to Ginger's relief, it stopped, and wheeling round, stared back over its tracks. Ginger reached for his rifle and stood ready for trouble. None came, however. The rhino may have caught his taint, for it wheeled again, and after staring at him for a few seconds went off at a gallop, grunting and squealing in its irritation at having been disturbed. Ginger was thankful to see it go. He had plenty to think about, without rhinos.

He was now too wide awake even to think of sleeping, so he sat down, rifle across his knee, to wait for dawn, or whatever else might befall. After what had happened he was prepared for almost anything. Or so he thought.

What actually happened next was, Mishu arrived at the double. It was then getting on for morning. The Masai appeared from nowhere, as the saying is, and his sudden appearance did nothing to steady Ginger's nerves, already at full stretch.

Mishu's manner was alert and his speech terse. Pointing in the direction of the scrub he said one word. "Cetezulu!"

"I saw him," answered Ginger. "How did you know?"

Mishu's answer explained his long absence. On arriving

32

at the nearest kraal he had learned at once that Cetezulu was coming up the side of the lake. Some members of his tribe returning from hunting brought the news. He had waited to confirm it. Indeed, he had done more than that. He had trailed the raiders to their hiding-place, which was in the clump of mixed scrub and trees. It was said that they had used the place before. He had watched them go in, and after making sure that they were not going to continue their journey that night, he had returned to Ginger to report. That was all.

There was no longer any doubt in Ginger's mind as to what he should do. As soon as it was light enough to see he would return to Kampala and tell Biggles. Cetezulu would hear him take off. He might take fright and bolt. But he would not be able to escape observation on the open ground in daylight. In four hours Biggles would be on the spot with the Mosquito. If the Black Elephant remained in cover he could be winkled out of it. Apart from air reconnaissance, now that Cetezulu's line of march was known it would be impossible for a large body of men to travel without leaving a trail for an expert tracker like Mishu to follow. It looked, thought Ginger optimistically, as if the Black Elephant had made his last raid.

Camp was broken and everything packed in the Auster ready for a quick take-off. Ginger watched the sky impatiently for the first streak of daylight. For something to do he got Mishu to help him to swing the tail of the machine so that its nose was pointing, as near as he could judge, over its landing-track. There were no obstructions there, and as there was still no sign of a breeze the direction of the take-off didn't matter. Upon such trivial details do vital events depend; for had the machine not been moved the story might have had a different ending.

With the first grey streak of the false dawn the temperature dropped sharply; and this produced a thin ground mist to blur the scene. Ginger was not unduly concerned. He thought it might delay him for a few minutes, that was all. For he knew that these conditions were quite normal and the mist would be dispersed by the first rays of the sun. And so it transpired. As the sun topped the horizon the mist began to rise like steam, disappearing as it rose.

Ginger took a last look at the copse wherein the Black Elephant and his followers were resting. Nothing moved; but revealed by the vanishing mist, standing at graze about two hundred yards away, was a magnificent gemsbok, its graceful tapering horns rising more than a yard above the conspicuous black and white markings on its face. Ginger paused to admire it, for the beast made a fine picture.

He was turning away when a rifle shot shattered the silence. The gemsbok went down as if struck by lightning. It was on its feet again in an instant, galloping madly towards the very spot where Ginger stood. It was not this that froze him stiff with shock, for as far as the animal was concerned he stood in no danger. It was what followed. From the grass beyond where the gazelle had been standing sprang a man, an enormous native, who, from the rifle he held, had fired the shot. And he was not alone. Beyond him appeared half a dozen others, who dashed forward in pursuit of their mortally wounded quarry. So far they had not seen anything else, but it would not be long before they did.

The gemsbok, blood frothing from its nostrils, tore past Ginger within a score of paces. In its blind panic it paid no attention to him, or the aircraft. But that, Ginger realised, would not be the case with its pursuers. He moved quickly. A shout told him that he had been seen. Mishu, true to his trade, was by this time at Ginger's elbow, rifle held ready, apparently prepared to fight. Ginger had no such intention. With one or two men to deal with the situation would have been different. Seven were too many.

"In you get!" he shouted, and scrambled into his seat.

The next half-minute was pandemonium. The engine came to life as Mishu fell into his seat and slammed the door, nearly spearing Ginger with his assegai in doing so.

The next moment the Auster was tearing tail-up through the grass on a course that was not quite as straight as it should have been. What was happening behind Ginger did not know. He didn't look to see. He was too taken up with what he was doing, and the fact that he was asking for disaster by running a stone-cold engine on full-throttle. The machine yawed sickeningly as he swerved to avoid an anthill, and he thought his undercarriage must go. But it stood up to the strain. Then, straight in front, a lioness with two cubs stood up to see what was coming. Ginger lifted the machine over them. It was all he could do. For a ghastly moment it seemed as if the Auster must stall. For a second or two it appeared to hang with its airscrew clawing at the air; then it picked up and the danger was past. Ginger, limp and white from strain, relaxed in his seat.

Reaching a safe height he turned slowly and looked down. The natives were standing still staring up at him. Some others had come out of the scrub. Of the animal that had caused the trouble, nothing could be seen, although it must be admitted that Ginger wasted no time looking for it. He was too shaken by the speed at which the whole thing had happened and the narrowness of his escape. He shuddered as he realised that had the lioness not stood up he must have crashed straight into her and her family, with results it were better not to think about.

That the Black Elephant might leave his hiding-place so early in the morning was a possibility that had not occurred to him—he didn't know why, because there was no reason why the man should remain in cover. The rest was easy to surmise. When the mist lifted Cetezulu must have seen the gemsbok and decided to stalk it, either for fresh meat or for the mere love of killing. Had the Auster not been ready for an instant take-off he would no doubt have killed more than the gemsbok.

What effect the sudden appearance of the aircraft would have on the raiders' plans was a matter for conjecture, but it seemed likely that they would draw the obvious conclusion. Cetezulu would realise that he had been seen, and in all probability, recognised. In that case he would not be likely to linger in the locality.

Running on full throttle Ginger made flat out for Kampala. His one fear was that Biggles might have left the ground for a reconnaissance on his own account.

This turned out not to be the case. Biggles and the others must have heard him coming, for they were on the airfield to meet him. Ginger taxied up to them and jumped down.

"You're soon back," greeted Biggles, a question in his tone of voice.

"I've seen him!!" cried Ginger.

"Seen whom!"

"The Elephant."

Biggles stared. "Are you sure?"

"Of course I'm sure. At one time he was only a hundred yards away from me."

"I'd say he was even closer than that," said Biggles in a curious voice. Stepping forward he drew something from the rear of the fuselage, just below the elevators, and held it up. It was an assegai.

Ginger blinked. "By gosh! I didn't know that was there," he gasped.

"You'd have known about it had it cut your elevator control," said Biggles grimly.

"Or if it had struck a few feet further forward," put in Algy.

"Well, at any rate, we've got the blighter's toothpick," declared Bertie.

"Tell us what happened," requested Biggles.

Ginger complied, trying to be coherent.

"That's fine!" was all Biggles had to say when he had finished. "Let's get weaving. We know where he was. We'll soon see if he's still there." He walked towards the other machines.

CHAPTER 4

TRICKED

"How about letting the police know where he is?" suggested Algy, as they reached the Mosquito.

"I'd rather make sure we know exactly where he is before we do that," answered Biggles. "A few miles mean little in the air, but they make a lot of difference when you're on the floor. We should look silly if we brought a ground force all this way and then had to admit that the Elephant had pulled his disappearing trick. Never mind about the Auster, Ginger. It's too slow. We shan't need it, anyway. You and Algy can come with me in the Mosquito. Bertie can follow on in the Proctor with Mishu.

"What's the drill if we catch up with the blighter?" enquired Bertie. "Do we knock spots off him? Or do we just watch him?"

"We'll give him a rattle," replied Biggles. "He's done a lot of hunting. It's time he had a taste of what it feels like to be hunted."

"Absolutely," agreed Bertie. "I am with you every time. There's no future in kid glove stuff when you're dealing with cut-throats. No, by Jove!"

Inside a quarter of an hour both machines were in the air. Biggles, with Algy and Ginger, pushed on, squeezing every possible revolution out of his engines, with the result that the Proctor was soon a speck in the sky far behind.

The first uneasy feeling that the job of locating the enemy was not going to be just "a slice of cake" came over Ginger when, gazing ahead, he failed to pick up the Lake, although by his reckoning they should now be within sight of it. He couldn't understand it, for such a vast landmark could hardly be missed. Staring, he made out what appeared to be a layer of low cloud, or ground mist, which blotted out the ground. He couldn't understand this, either, for now that the sun was well up all such moisture should have been dissipated. Presently he conveyed his doubts to Biggles. "What's all that murk ahead?" he asked in a puzzled voice.

"Smoke," answered Biggles laconically. "It can't be anything else."

"Smoke!" echoed Ginger, still not understanding. "From what?"

"The grass," returned Biggles. "It's on fire. Natives may have done it in the ordinary way. They burn off the dead grass from time to time to encourage new growth. But somehow, I don't think that was the idea on this occasion. It would be too much like coincidence. I suspect that artful rogue, the Elephant, was responsible. It would be just the sort of trick that he would think of. That dry grass would burn like petrol, and run for miles. The deuce of it is, there's no wind to carry the smoke away."

Very soon there was no doubt about it. Smoke it was. It became possible to smell it, even at the two thousand feet at which the Mosquito was flying. Sometimes the fire itself could be seen ahead of the smoke, a two-mile-long river of yellow flame from which rolled up a great white cloud, in the form of an umbrella, many miles in diameter, completely concealing what lay below. Somewhere underneath the pall, Ginger had no doubt, was the Elephant, making a forced march to a more secure retreat.

"The scoundrel must have guessed you would recognise him, and took the tip to pull out," remarked Biggles.

For a minute, Ginger, in his disappointment and chagrin, didn't know what to say. The truth was all too clear. The Black Elephant, living up to his reputation, had been too smart for them. "By now, he'll be on his way out of the district," he opined, gloomily.

"He will—firing more grass as he goes," agreed Biggles. "And he'll go on doing that, no doubt, while he can hear aircraft, or until darkness makes it unnecessary."

He went on through the smoke to the lake. Here the

air was clear, of course, but its placid surface was unbroken by a mark of any sort. "There's no point in wasting time here," said Biggles, and turned back over his course.

There was nowhere else to look. The fire was spreading, giving the impression that the whole country was on fire. Great areas of charred earth, where the fire had burnt itself out although it was still smouldering, could be glimpsed through a quivering haze. Farther on, clear of the conflagration, animals of many sorts could be seen moving to safe ground.

"We might as well go back to base for all the good we're likely to do here," said Biggles at last. "Call Bertie and tell him it's no use. We'll rally on the airfield and talk about it."

The Mosquito retraced its course to Kampala. Bertie, who had turned the Proctor on receipt of Biggles's signal, touched down shortly afterwards. They all went to the bungalow where Biggles lit a cigarette and turned his attention to the map.

"What a miserable flop!" muttered Ginger disgustedly.

"Don't let it depress you," Biggles told him. "It was a wonderful stroke of luck to get on the track of the gang right away. To put a rope on the Elephant on the same day was rather a lot to expect. We've lost him for the moment. No matter. We know roughly where he is so it shouldn't be difficult to pick up his trail again. He has probably worked out by now that aircraft are looking for him, which in one way is a pity. On the other hand, it will keep him on the jump. Let him do his fifty miles a day. That won't help him much. We can do the same distance in ten minutes, and he knows it. That fact alone should give him something to think about."

"He may turn off now in another direction," said Algy.

"He may, but I don't think he will," answered Biggles thoughtfully. "That is, unless we press him too hard. He must have been working on a definite plan and I'd say he'll stick to it if he can. He may try to speed things up a bit, but that needn't worry us."

"The question is, old boy, what are we going to do about it right now?" asked Bertie, polishing his eyeglass.

"After we've had a bite of lunch we'll carry on with the hunt," Biggles told him. "I'm not going to sit here doing nothing. We know the Elephant was heading north. The chances are he'll keep going north. We'll cut across his track. Sooner or later we shall spot something to work on. I still think that somewhere in front of him there must be a big herd of looted cattle. He's not likely to abandon it. We'll keep an eye open for it."

"What about these smoke fires?" queried Ginger dubiously. "If he keeps up that game it will defeat us."

"On the contrary, it would, in the end, defeat him," asserted Biggles.

"How d'you make that out?"

"The smoke will tell us where he is, which is the last thing he'll want us to know. He's not such a fool that he won't realise that. He could afford to pull the trick this morning because he had nothing to lose by it. We already knew where he was. When he thinks he's given us the slip he'll think twice before he even lights a cooking-fire. Aside from that, he'll have to pass through country where it isn't possible to burn the ground. Africa isn't all grass. If he keeps going north it won't be long before he's in the big mountain country, and there he's likely to strike rain. It's the time of the year. Rain would put his fires out, even if he could light one. No, I'm not worried about his smoke trick."

"If he gets into the rain forests on the lower slopes of the Mitumba and Ruwenzori ranges we should have a nice job to find him, let alone winkle him out," muttered Algy.

"It may not be as difficult as all that," argued Biggles. "He couldn't get through the actual forests—certainly not with a herd of cattle. He'd have to follow native paths or game tracks. Naturally, we shall watch them. Have a good look at the map, all of you. It will give you an idea of what we shall be flying over presently if the Elephant continues to push on north. He may not get as far. We may be able to trim his tusks before he hits the mountains. Incidentally, he'll have to go through them, or round them. There's no question of getting over them. Some of them have never been climbed. Even in this part of the world the snow never melts above sixteen thousand feet, and some of these African pimples have snow on them all the year round. That should give you an idea of how high they are. But let's go and have a bite and we'll get on with the work."

Biggles said little during lunch. When the meal was finished he returned to the map, the others going with him. "I've been thinking about this business," he resumed. "In country of this size it's obviously going to be difficult to work to a time-table; but we shall have to adopt some sort of method or we're likely to go round in circles indefinitely. To rely on luck to hit the trail is too chancy. Very well. We know where the Elephant is, or was, this morning. We also know that he was heading north. We can safely assume that there was nothing haphazard about that. Our black friend knew where he was going. It's reasonable to suppose that he'll stick to his arrangements as long as it's possible. According to his previous operation he and his followers are due to fade out for a while, either to have a rest or dispose of their loot—possibly both. For this purpose they must have a hide-out. They can't keep moving all the time. Very well. Every time the Elephant has disappeared he was last heard of in Northern Uganda. I shall assume, therefore, that the hide-out is in that area, or to the north of it. At present he is well to the south of it. If our guess is right, it follows that he will continue to move north—as fast as possible no doubt, if he has realised that we are after him."

"That may induce him to make a detour," suggested Algy.

"I think he will have to be forced pretty hard before he'll do that," declared Biggles. "To turn east would mean

41

forcing a passage through the sheer jungle of the Belgian Congo. To veer west would mean entering the more thickly populated regions near Lake Victoria. Between these areas lies the West Rift Valley, which, as you can see from the map here, lies more or less in the shadow of big mountain systems. He's not likely to tackle those. There's another reason why he'll stick to the valley, which brings me back to my old argument. He'll need water for the cattle. Through the valley he has a string of lakes— Kiva, Edward, George and Albert. At the far end he strikes the Victoria Nile—water all the way. I'm convinced that is the route Cetezulu intended to take, and he'll stick to it if he can. Anyway, I shall work on that assumption and start watching that line of country. Our westerly limit will be the mountains. They're roughly a hundred and fifty to two hundred miles from where we stand here. The area to be watched is about five hundred miles long, so it will mean a lot of work. The thing to look for is a big herd, or several small herds, of cattle, moving north. We can photograph anything that looks suspicious and examine it at home under the magnifying-glass."

"Why not try to pin him down at the northern end of Lake Tanganyika?" suggested Ginger. "He can't have got as far as that yet."

"Because that's just what he'd expect us to do," answered Biggles. "By putting up that smoke-screen he has virtually told us that he knows he's been spotted, and that being so he'll play foxy until he thinks he's out of the danger zone—lying in thick cover all day and moving fast by night, as he has on previous occasions. We can suppose that he knows every inch of the ground, having been over it several times before. It would require an army of men to form a cordon through which he couldn't pass without being seen. No, our only chance of spotting him is from up topsides, and the best opportunities for that will come when he thinks he's safe and tries to make up for lost time."

Biggles turned to Mishu, who was standing by, following the conversation intently. "What do you think about it, Mishu?" he enquired.

The Masai answered that he agreed with all Biggles had said. They were, he averred, words of wisdom. But as he knew nothing about aeroplanes, and didn't care for flying, he suggested that it would be better if he could be taken to Northern Uganda where he knew not only the game trails but most of the people. He could be left there, and by moving about the native villages would certainly learn of the approach of the Black Elephant, should he evade the air patrols. The natives might be afraid to mention Cetezulu to a white man for fear of reprisals, but they would talk among themselves. He, by listening to their conversation, would pick up any news. He felt sure that Cetezulu would sooner or later pass through Northern Uganda, for one of his hiding-places was the elephant-grass where his master, Major Harvey, had been killed. There was a Government landing-ground there, with a rest-house, near a kraal named Latonga. He could be landed there. Afterwards, the aeroplane could fly up sometimes to see if he had any news. He was quite sure that Cetezulu would not be able to pass that way without him knowing about it.

This was such a sensible plan that Biggles agreed to it forthwith. In the ordinary way, Mishu, knowing nothing of air observation, would merely be so much extra weight to carry. If he was needed for a specific job he could always be brought back.

The upshot of the conference, then, was this. Mishu would be planted at Latonga, on the Black Elephant's presumed route northward, while the aircraft would maintain contact with him between a regular schedule of watching the wild territory in the region of the West Rift Valley.

"You might as well take Mishu up right away," Biggles told Ginger. "We shall then be all clear to start a reconnaissance shuttle-service tomorrow morning. Take the Auster and fly a compass course to Latonga. It isn't much

43

more than a couple of hundred miles so you should get back easily before sundown."

"Fair enough," agreed Ginger, glad to have something to do, and proceeded forthwith to carry out the order.

In twenty minutes he was in the air, with Mishu as passenger, heading northward over the dry, sparsely-wooded terrain that had become familiar. The weather was fine, and appeared to be settled, so he expected no difficulty. Nor was he disappointed, and in due course he set his passenger down on the rough Government landing-ground. It took him a few minutes to locate the actual landing-strip, as the whole area was in the nature of a plain and the only identification marks consisted of a white circle, largely overgrown, a tattered wind-stocking on a dead thorn tree, and the rest-house, which happened to be half concealed under some acacia scrub. However, after circling for a little while he spotted the white ring which told him all he needed to know. Mishu got out of the machine and waved good-bye; and Ginger was about to take off again forthwith when there occurred one of those incidents, apparently trivial at the time, which can have results so far-reaching, so catastrophic, that not by any stretch of the imagination could they be foreseen.

CHAPTER 5

VISIBILITY ZERO

OUT of the rest-house, a primitive-looking building comprising a single long room with a thatched roof and an earth floor, stepped a white man, a youngish man dressed in the conventional tropical kit of a white hunter in Central Africa. It was well worn and had obviously seen a lot of hard work, so Ginger, who naturally got out of the machine to pass the time of day, was not surprised to learn that the stranger was, in fact, an assistant game ranger. His name was Simmonds, and it turned out that he had been sent to the locality to deal with a leopard which, according to a complaint, had advanced from cattle-raiding to attacking human beings. Simmonds had been there for three days but so far he had seen nothing of the leopard. He still hoped to get on terms with the beast.

Ginger, of course, stayed on to have a chat, in the first place to ascertain if the game ranger had heard anything of the Black Elephant (which he had not) and later, over a cup of tea, to listen to a recital of the strange things that cap happen to a man who spends his life among African big game. Simmonds told him that there was still a lot of poaching going on in the district, notably of elephant and rhino; and he was afraid that it would continue until the people primarily responsible, the unscrupulous traders who bought the ivory, were laid by the heels. The native population would of course do nothing to help, as they profited by these transactions. Simmonds was of the opinion that somewhere in the background there was a white man who was the real cause of the nuisance.

The outcome of all this was, Ginger dallied much longer than he intended. In fact, it was only when he noticed some heavy clouds rolling down from the north-east that he looked at his watch and realised how much time had slipped past unnoticed. Mishu had disappeared, so, after thanking his host for his hospitality and wishing him good hunting, he walked briskly to the Auster, took off and headed south.

Up to this point he was not in the least concerned either with the time he had lost, which after all was unimportant since he had nothing else to do, or with the approaching storm clouds, even though they were beginning to look ugly. If they overtook him—well, he had flown through storms before, and expected nothing worse than a buffeting with reduced visibility. If any blame could be attached to him for what followed it was the result of this confidence. Where he was at fault, as he was soon to tell himself, was in failing to notice a change in the direction of the wind, and its velocity. In short, he omitted to check his drift until the mischief had been done.

The storm was upon him before he perceived, with the first twinge of alarm, that it was no ordinary affair, either in size or violence. A mighty mass of towering cumulus, indigo in colour and lacerated by forks of lightning, came bearing down on him from almost due east. Even before it struck him he knew that he was in for trouble, for the pressure of air being packed and thrust before the mass of moisture began to toss the light aircraft about as if it had been a feather. The engine groaned in protest.

Ginger looked down hurriedly in the hope of seeing a landmark that he could recognise. There was none. What was worse, he had an uncomfortable feeling that the ground was new to him. It was much rougher than anything he had seen on the way out. Confirmation of this came when, before the storm blotted out everything, he observed that his westward drift was nearly as fast as his forward speed. How long he had been drifting he did not know, but it was obvious that he must be many miles off his course. By this time he was more than a little worried. And when, to cap all, he remembered that he had not "topped-up" his tanks before taking off, his alarm moved nearer to fear. Already he was running on his auxiliary tank. He found small consolation in the fact that in normal conditions he would have had an ample margin of petrol. He began to look at his gauge, already low, more often.

His compass was now swinging wildly, so in what direction he was actually travelling he did not know. His nose pointed to the east, or what he thought was the east; but not knowing the speed or the direction of the storm, which might be cyclonic, he was by no means sure of it. Aside from that, it was soon taking him all his time to keep the machine on even keel. Again and again the control column was nearly wrenched from his hand as a blast of air struck the underside of a wing and threatened to turn him over. The sensation was as if he was sailing on invisible mountainous seas. He could no longer see anything except dark grey mist tearing past, so he was not always sure of the position of the aircraft in relation to the ground. Thunder boomed, drowning the drone of the motor. Lightning illuminated the cabin with a ghastly glare.

There is a common impression that airmen fear nothing: that they take this sort of thing as all part of the day's work: that they battle with meteorological phenomena with a song on their lips: that they have all the equipment necessary to deal with such emergencies. True, modern machines are well equipped, but the cold-blooded employment of it when the aircraft is being blown about like a scrap of thistle-down, is not so easy as it might appear from text books on the subject. No, the truth is, in such conditions as those in which Ginger now found himself, most pilots are badly shaken, and wish fervently that they were safely on the ground.

Ginger was, and he would have been the first to admit it, scared rigid, as he had every reason to be, for he was well aware that he was fighting for his life. Not only was he exceedingly doubtful about the outcome of it, but there was really very little that he could do about it. Forces outside his control had him in their grip, and whether or not he survived was largely a matter of chance. All he could do was keep his head and hope for the best. With plenty of air space, and fuel, it would have been bad enough; but having little of either he was white to the lips with strain and anxiety. He knew he was far to the westward of his true course, and in that direction, as Biggles had so recently explained, lay the big mountains. As an airman might put it, the clouds around him might be expected to have rocks in them. Mount Stanley, nearly seventeen thousand feet, could not be far away. With his limited fuel supply he couldn't hope to get above it. His altimeter, set for Kampala, registered seven thousand feet.

The thought of Kampala reminded him that he ought

to try to let Biggles know what was happening, if he could make contact, which seemed doubtful in view of the distance he was from his base plus the electrical disturbances of the storm. He soon gave it up as hopeless. Any signals, which at such a range would be weak, were drowned in the vicious crackles of the electrical discharges that were going on around him.

For what he judged to be about twenty minutes, although it may have been less, he battled his way through the heart of a tropical storm of a violence beyond his experience. He could see nothing, above, around or below, except billowing masses of grey vapour racing past his cockpit. From time to time, rain, and hail, lashed the aircraft like a thousand whips, with a noise that made him wince. It amazed him that the machine could take such a pounding and still hold together.

Then, slowly, as if with reluctance, it became lighter. This told him that he was through the worst and gave him new hope. He was, of course, still striving to get back to somewhere near his proper course, although he knew that it must now be far to the westward of his position. Staring ahead through the streaming windscreen he saw what appeared to be another mass of cloud bearing down on him. It was an unusual triangular shape, and very dark. Only at the last moment did he realise that it was too dense to be a cloud; that it was in fact a mountain into which he was flying. Cold from shock he swung away and saw the mass glide past his wing tip like a monstrous apparition. This settled any doubt as to his position. He was in the mountains. His eyes switched to his petrol gauge. The needle was down to zero. At any moment the engine would cut, and then, whatever the result, he would have to go down. There was no longer any hope of climbing out of danger.

Quickly he decided to save his last drop of petrol for dire emergency. He throttled back, eased the joy-stick forward, and began to glide. He had to brace himself to do it, for, still flying "blind," he had no idea of how far he could go without colliding with the earth. The altimeter was useless. It still registered seven thousand feet of height, but that made no allowance for mountains. For all he knew he might be within fifty feet of the ground. Holding his breath and straining his eyes he went on, praying that he might see an obstruction, should there be one on his line of flight, before he hit it. Twice, dimly, on either side, he saw ominous shadows in the cloud slide past. Another rose before him, forcing him to open up again.

For perhaps another two minutes the engine maintained its customary note. Then it spluttered. It cut out, came on for another few seconds, spluttered again, and then cut, as Ginger knew, for the last time. The airscrew came to rest. He held straight on, which was all he could do, in an uncanny silence, broken only by the boom of distant thunder. For what seemed an eternity of time he stared down into the opaque bowl below him, waiting for the end.

It came slowly. The mist seemed to harden. It became deeper, more solid, in colour. Then, through it, appeared a phantom world of uneven ground from which sprang stunted, misshapen trees and giant weeds. Easing the control column back as near as he dared to stalling point he floated down into them. At the last instant he flicked off the ignition and flattened out for a pancake landing. As the aircraft began to sink bodily he lifted his knees to his chin to prevent his legs from being trapped, covered his face with his arms, and waited for the inevitable crash. The machine checked, shuddering, as the undercarriage was wiped off. The safety-belt tightened on his stomach like an iron band. Then, with a splintering of wood and rending of fabric the Auster bored into some bushes, flinging him against the instrument panel. It tilted on its nose, and then, quite slowly sank back. Silence fell.

Panting from shock Ginger scrambled out and stumbled into a sitting position on a pile of wet moss. And there for some minutes he sat, trembling from the shock of his ordeal but unscathed except for a bump on the forehead where it had struck the instrument board; but above all, he was wonderfully relieved to find that he was still alive.

With the loss of his machine he was not at that moment particularly concerned. All that mattered was, he was safely on the ground in one piece. It induced that almost overwhelming feeling of thankfulness that most pilots experience at least once in their careers—unless they are very lucky.

After a little while, feeling more normal, he took stock of his position. It was not encouraging. As far as he could make out, visibility was still confined to not much more than a hundred yards, he was on a rough plateau. One end of it fell away into a cauldron of mist. On the other three sides the ground rose sharply into the murk to an unknown height. He had only a vague idea of where he was in relation to his base. All he knew for certain was, he was well to the west of it. The last time he had looked at his altimeter it had registered between six and seven thousand feet, so he supposed that he was lodged somewhere in the mountains at that height. The shrubs, and herbage, were unlike anything he had seen before. He took them to be the ordinary plants of the African higher altitude.

The heavy rain had given way to a dreary drizzle. Darkness was closing in. Deciding that there was no sense in getting wet, and perceiving that there was nothing he could do for the time being, he got back into the cabin, which was still more or less in one piece, to think things over in less discomfort. One thing was evident. The aircraft would never fly again. Nor would it be possible for another machine to land anywhere near him, even supposing that he was located by Biggles, which seemed by no means certain. If ever he was to get home it looked as if he would have to walk—a prospect that depressed, but did not particularly dismay him.

The first thing to do, obviously, was to let the others know where he was and what had happened, if that could be done. It was a big if. The radio did not appear to have suffered any damage, but the range was long and he was not sure how the instrument would behave on the ground. Against that he had altitude, which might help. Signals would in any case be weak, he thought; not that that would matter if he could make contact. Biggles would know by now that he must be down somewhere, although he would be unable to do anything about it until the morning.

He reached for the instrument and went to work, sending out his call sign; but all he got back was such a crackle of atmospherics, due presumably to the proximity of the electrical storm, that he soon gave up rather than risk weakening his battery which, without an engine, could not be recharged. It would be better to wait until the air cleared.

Making himself as comfortable as possible in the cramped cockpit, he settled down to wait. The storm passed, although he could still hear it in the distance. Visibility improved. The moon appeared, to reveal a magnificent if rather frightening spectacle of mountain scenery. It was, Ginger thought, like being in another world. That was his last conscious impression. Tired out, he dozed off to sleep.

CHAPTER 6

AN ILLUMINATING DISCOVERY

NOT until a flush in the eastern sky announced the approach of another day did Ginger wake up, to discover that he was stiff with cold. Wherefore he stamped up and down for some minutes to restore life to his numbed limbs before tackling the radio again. To his great satisfaction he soon picked up a voice which, although faint, he recognised as Algy's. Algy told him to hold on while he fetched Biggles.

When Biggles came, Ginger, still conserving his battery, told him as quickly and as briefly as possible what had happened. He could not give his exact position, of course, but he could state his approximate altitude, which would be a guide. He also gave the time of his departure from Latonga. This, together with the direction and the velocity of the storm, which Biggles had seen, would be another indication. He told Biggles there could be no question of landing. The Auster was a "write-off". He was unhurt and was prepared to walk home, or to the nearest point where he could be picked up.

Biggles told him to stay where he was until he had found him and dropped him some stores. He thought that by following the seven thousand-foot contour it should not be difficult. He would start right away in the Proctor. If Ginger heard the machine he was to light a smudge fire to show his position. That was all.

Feeling better Ginger got out to thaw in the welcome warmth of the rising sun, and survey the landscape in the broad light of day. It looked like being a fine one.

As the sun banished the last shreds of morning mist a magnificent panorama was revealed, had he been in the mood to appreciate it. He was, as he suspected, on the broad shoulder of a mountain which rose behind and above him to a snow-capped peak. To the east, the ground fell sharply to the timber line, about a thousand feet below, where, in a more gentle gradient, the scrub met the great rain forest, which persisted until it merged into the brown face of the Central African tableland. At the base of the last foothill, a bright green band, like the hem of a skirt, was conspicuous. He noticed it without troubling to wonder what it was. Far to the north, the sun glittered on a big sheet of water. For the rest, he was too far away to make out any details. There was no sign of life, near or far; not even a bird. It struck him that he might well be the first human being to stand on that precise spot.

By the time he had finished his survey, tidied himself and munched a bar of chocolate from his iron rations, he heard the sound for which he was waiting; the purr, still distant, of an aircraft. Forthwith he set about lighting a fire to make smoke to show his position. This was by no means an easy matter, as everything was soaking wet. However, with some unused pages from the engine log-book, and some torn fabric dipped in oil, he succeeded in sending a column of smoke into the motionless air.

The drone of the Proctor drew nearer, faded, and then came on again. It was some time before he saw it. When he did, it appeared round a flank of the mountain slightly above him. Almost at once it turned in his direction, the pilot obviously having seen the smoke. Ginger stood in a conspicuous position and waved. The Proctor made two low circuits round him. Then it climbed a little, and coming in on a short run, dropped a fairly bulky parcel attached to what was clearly a home-made parachute. The bundle struck the ground not far from the crashed Auster. Ginger collected it and found, wrapped in a water-proof sheet, a miscellaneous collection of stores and equipment likely to be useful to him. It comprised, among other things, tins of jam, meat, biscuits and condensed milk, packed into a rucksack. There was a rifle, cart-ridges, pocket-compass, hatchet, first-aid outfit and mos-quito repellent. There was also a note from Biggles.

He sat down to read it. It was, as he expected, brief and explicit. He was to start walking down the mountain, keeping always to the east. If he failed to get through the forest before nightfall he was to light a fire to show how much progress he had made. No fire would be taken to mean that he had met with an accident. It would not be possible to see him while he was in the forest, but smoke would rise above the trees. When he reached open ground on which it was possible to make a landing, the Proctor would pick him up.

Ginger waved to show that he understood, whereupon the Proctor turned away, heading south-east, presumably for Kampala. There was, Ginger realised, nothing more it could do, so there was no point in it hanging about over such dangerous country.

He made a substantial meal and set off on his long journey, setting a course on the line taken by the Proctor. With the pack on his back and the rifle under his arm he began a long traverse towards the timber-line, picking his way carefully, aware that even a minor accident could have calamitous results. On the whole the going was fairly easy, if rough. The hard labour, he suspected, would begin when he reached the forest. And it did. He had had some experience of tropical rain forests so he was not surprised to find himself confronted by an interlaced tangle of vegetation which at first sight appeared to be impenetrable. The very magnitude of the task of getting through it may have been his salvation, for in walking along the fringe, looking for an opening, thinking that he might find a place where a landslide had cut a gap in the trees, he came upon a game track. From the churned-up state of the glutinous mud it appeared to be in regular use, which made him pause for a moment, for there was obviously some risk in using it, particularly as in the event of an encounter neither he nor the beast would be able to turn aside. However, he decided that as the path would save him hours of time, and untold labour, it was a risk worth taking. He took the precaution of loading his rifle, and with the safety catch on, plunged into the dim labyrinth that fell away before him.

He made good progress although the mud was tiresome, often causing him to slip. The flies, too, were a nuisance, although he applied repellent to his face with a lavish hand. The air became increasingly heavy and oppressive. Occasionally he passed a place where the undergrowth had been trampled flat by the beasts that used the path. He approached such spots warily, stopping often to listen; but seeing and hearing nothing he pressed on, determined to get the business over as quickly as possible. It began to look as if he was alone in the forest after all.

It was about lunch time that he was provided with evidence that this was not the case. He was, he judged, about a third of the way down, and coming upon a mysterious-looking pool that would provide him with a drink, cast about for a dry spot on which to sit while he made a quick meal. To the left, and slightly above him, there was a narrow glade, caused, it appeared, by a rock face behind it. It was deep in coarse weeds, but he made his way towards it hoping that there would be fewer flies than there were under the trees. He found a large rock which had fallen from above, and he was about to seat himself on it preparatory to unloading his rucksack when a movement caught his eye. Out of the rough herbage, about fifty yards away, rose an animal which hitherto he had seen only in captivity. It was a gorilla. The beast had evidently been bending down, but now that it stood erect it was in plain view. In its huge fist it held a root of what looked like celery. It bit a piece off the end and started munching.

Ginger, while not particularly alarmed, for he had always understood that these animals were not pugnacious unless molested, began to back away rather than have any argument about the ownership of the place; and in this he may have made a mistake, for the movement, slight though it was, was noticed immediately. The gorilla stopped chewing, mouth open, and stared. But not for long. Apparently it took a violent dislike to Ginger on sight, and with a roar of rage it hurled the celery aside and charged.

Ginger, realising that flight would not save him, dropped everything he was carrying except the rifle. By the time he had slipped off the safety catch, the beast was almost on him. In his frantic haste he fired wildly, knowing, even as the pulled the trigger that he was not on his target. The bullet went wide. But the flash, or the report, or the yell that he let out, may have served an even more useful purpose, for the great ape turned aside and went plunging on down into the forest, leaving Ginger reloading feverishly. It did not return. For a while Ginger stood motionless, badly scared, listening to the diminishing sounds of the animal's retreat. With a hand that was not quite steady he mopped his face with a handkerchief already filthy, and then retraced his steps to the game track. Not liking the locality he went on a little way until, finding a fallen tree, he sat down to have his lunch, wondering if he had ever really been in serious danger from the animal. Anyway, he hoped there were no more. He had no desire to put the matter to the test.

He did not eat much—a few biscuits smeared with jam. He was too hot, and too anxious to get out of the timber. He hoped to be out of it before nightfall, but was doubtful.

Four o'clock found him on what he thought must be the lower slopes, but he could not be sure of this, for the trees that hemmed him in on all sides prevented him from getting a clear view. But the character of the forest had been changing, slowly for some time. Palms and ferns began to appear. There were brooks, too, to be forded. The game track had several times been crisscrossed by others, and fresh marks everywhere warned him to be on the look-out. He saw where elephants had been feeding, stripping the branches from young trees, within the last few hours. However, he pushed on, using his compass to keep him on a course as straight as the state of the ground would allow. The trees began to thin.

An open glade, with at last a clear view ahead, brought him to a halt. He had been hoping for some time to get an idea of how much farther he had to go, and what the conditions on the lower ground were like. What he saw did nothing to cheer him up. True, the timber for the last half-mile became ever more open and offered a comparatively easy passage; but beyond that was the bright green strip that he had observed from above. He now saw that it was a broad expanse of bamboo swamp, caused obviously by water draining down from above. Whether or not the ground was firm, or actual bog, he did not know, and had no means of telling. What he did know was that it skirted the entire eastern base of the mountain, many miles of it, so there could be no question of going round it. Beyond it he could see a fringe of elephant-grass, but that didn't worry him.

The sun was already low, and he realised gloomily that he could abandon any hope of getting on to open ground that night. Indeed, he was by no means sure that unless the bamboo was traversed by game tracks he would get through it the next day, either. He was well plastered with mud, and very tired, and he had looked forward to having a rest; but in the circumstances he resolved to carry on at least as far as the bamboo in order to satisfy himself that it was passable. Once, some time before, he had thought he had heard an aircraft; but he was near a noisy brook at the time, and the nearer sound drowned all others. In any case he could not have lit a fire, as everything in the forest was waterlogged. In the more open ground ahead he expected to find some dry brushwood, so this difficulty would not arise. Wearily, he strode on.

He was now in typical lion country, but he saw none. The only animals he saw were a rhino and some waterbuck. They were some way off and moved away at his approach. It was a relief to be out of the dismal forest, anyway, he told himself as he slogged down the last slopes to the bamboo belt. Nearing it, noticing what he thought was a fair place to make camp, he dropped his load and went on to the last obstacle. It proved to be an even more difficult one than he had expected. The ground was reasonably firm, but the knotty stems of the bamboo stood so close together that getting through them was cleary going to be a long and tedious business. It would, he decided, be folly to risk being benighted in such a jungle. The job would be bad enough in daylight. He looked for game tracks, but found none, although he felt sure there must be some.

Thinking the matter over, he recalled, when he was looking at the place from above, seeing a spot where the green belt narrowed considerably for a short distance; but whether it was to the left of him, or the right, he had no idea. Nor had he any notion how far he was away from it. He regretted now that he had not paid more attention to it; but then, at that time, he did not even know what it was. He looked again at the barrier. The stems of the plants were not thick, perhaps an inch or so in diameter, but they grew in a dense mass and were fully twenty feet high. There was no break anywhere.

He was testing them to ascertain how easily they could be pushed aside, to permit a passage through them, when, from no great distance away, in the swamp, there came a sound, an animal sound, that made him stop abruptly. He took it to be a buffalo, bellowing; and the first thought that occurred to him was, naturally, if there were animals there, then there must be tracks. The thought of invading an area occupied by buffalo, perhaps the most dangerous animals in Africa, was not pleasant; but eventually, if not then, the prospect would have to be faced. He reckoned there was still about twenty minutes of daylight left, so picking up his rifle he started forcing a passage into the swamp with the intention of ascertaining there and then if there were any tracks. If there were it would be a load off his mind. He had no fear of failing to find his way back for his passage left a track of crumpled reeds.

It was a strange world in which he found himself, a world composed of nothing but bamboos. The slim stems and long green leaves surrounded him on all sides and formed a trellis over his head. But he soon forgot all about this when he succeeded in his quest beyond all expectation. Without warning he broke suddenly into a veritable cavern in the crowding vegetation. At least, it struck him as a cavern, or a tunnel, because, although the track was the best part of thirty feet wide, the canes on each side had bent over under the weight of their feathery tops to meet overhead, thus forming an arched corridor.

Ginger stared at this fantastic highway in amazement. He couldn't understand it. Only an enormous herd of buffaloes could have made such a track, and he had been under the impression that the great herds that once roamed Africa existed no longer. None was in sight, although some had been there recently, for there were fresh droppings everywhere. Indeed, he could smell the beasts and, of course, he had heard one bellow, so they could not be far away.

Still standing there, staring, a light-coloured object lying beside the track not far away aroused his curiosity, and he walked forward cautiously to investigate it. It was, he found, a hide; the hide of a calf, recently dead. The blood on it was still red. The hoofs were worn, as if with hard travelling. But the significance of these details was overwhelmed by another, one which gave Ginger his first suspicion of the truth. The hide was brown and white. It was not the skin of a buffalo. It was the coat of a young domestic cow. The flesh had been eaten and the hide discarded. The explanation was so obvious that it hit Ginger like a thunderclap, as the saying is. He remembered that he was in the West Rift Valley, which followed the base of the mountains. He understood now why there were no jagged stumps of bamboos at his feet. Dropping on his knees he confirmed it. The bamboos had been *cut*. Cut flush with the ground. The whole thing was artificial, man-made. And the man who had caused it to be made, Ginger knew, without a shadow of doubt, was the Black Elephant. This was the way he came. This was the secret track up which he drove his stolen cattle, screened from all sides, and from above. No wonder he could vanish at will!

Ginger looked at his compass. The road ran almost due north and south—the direction, of course, of the Rift Valley. Hoof-prints showed that a herd of cattle had lately moved north. Biggles had been right. The cattle, if not the raiders, were moving northward. There must, Ginger reasoned, be two parties. The Black Elephant's personal mob of thieves and murderers and a body of men in charge of the stolen cattle.

All weariness banished by this momentous discovery, Ginger hastened back to the place where he had struck the road, and lost no time in removing himself from it. Knowing what the result would be if he were found on it he made his way back to his proposed camp, slightly breathless, to digest the startling information on which he had stumbled. He was now more than ever anxious to make contact with Biggles, but he could not see how this was to be achieved. Biggles! The light was fast fading, but there was still time for him to come over for a final reconnaissance to learn how far he, Ginger, had got.

Hardly had the thought struck him than he heard the machine coming. This threw him into a quandary. Light a fire he dared not, for fear the smoke was seen by Cetezulu's men, some of who, he felt sure, were not far away. Moreover, if he did light a fire, the chances were that Biggles would circle low to have a look at him. This again could hardly fail to arouse the curiosity of Cetezulu's gang. On the other hand, if he did not light a fire, Biggles would, as he had in fact said, assume that he had met with an accident. In that case he would soon be along on foot to find him, with results that might also be catastrophic.

In the end Ginger did nothing. He heard the machine go on—indeed he saw it, fairly high up; but he made no signal. It was a risk he dared not take. What he would do in the morning he did not know; but he would at least have time to think the matter over. The aircraft circled for a while, getting farther and farther away. Then the drone faded and he heard it no more.

Deep night settled on the scene. A long way off a lion roared. For some time Ginger sat with his rifle across his knees, listening for sounds of movement on the secret road. If men or cattle were there it should be possible to hear them, he thought. Much now depended on it. However, no sounds came. Presently, with difficulty, he collected some dry brushwood, so that he could light a fire quickly should any nocturnal prowlers behave threateningly. If any appeared he did not see them. He munched some biscuits without enjoying them, eyes always alert. The night wore on. Still no sounds came from the track through the bamboo. Men, he reasoned, might move silently; but not cattle. He came to the conclusion that the beast he had heard was one of a drove that had gone through. Finally he risked a little fire, as much for its cheerful company as for any other reason. After a while he dozed.

CHAPTER 7

A BUSY MORNING

DAWN found Ginger on his feet, still tired after a troubled night but anxious to be moving. He made a quick breakfast and disposed of the empty cans by sinking them in a nearby brook, where he also had a drink and a rub down with a wet handkerchief. Feeling somewhat better he got his kit ready for marching, and then stood ready to signal to Biggles, whom he felt sure would come over at least once more in the aircraft before taking other steps to locate him.

In the absence of any sound from the bamboo track he had already decided to light a smoke fire when he heard the machine. If there was no such signal, Biggles would, he knew, soon be searching for him on foot; and for more reasons than one he was anxious to prevent this, which might well lead to serious trouble for everyone. Moving to the most open place he could find, he made a little pile of dry grass and brushwood and then sat down to watch the sky. Biggles would, he thought, realise that it was the bamboo swamp that was holding him up; but he would know nothing about the secret track no matter how low he came over it.

He had not long to wait. The sun was only just clear of the horizon when he heard a machine, and recognised the deep-throated drone of the Mosquito. Putting a match to the fire he had prepared he had the satisfaction of seeing a thin pillar of white smoke coil upwards in the still air. This was soon observed, and the machine arrived over the spot, banking steeply as it circled. Ginger stood up and waved to show that he was all right. There was nothing more that he could do. The Mosquito continued to circle, and presently a tobacco tin came whistling down. He fetched it, and opening it, took out the note which he knew it would contain. It read: *"Move three miles south. Swamp narrows. Will wait for you on far side. B."*

Ginger waved again to show that he understood, stamped out the fire, picked up his kit and was soon on his way, feeling that at last things were beginning to look brighter. The aircraft droned away, presumably to land on the far side of the narrow part of the swamp, and there await his arrival.

As he strode along the thought occurred to him that if any of Cetezulu's men did happen to be anywhere near, they would not fail to notice the plane, and its curious behaviour. They would certainly watch it, and watching it would see the smoke, in which case, by putting two and two together, they could hardly fail to arrive at the correct answer. Should that happen they would come to investigate. Wherefore he not only kept a watchful eye on the edge of the swamp but struck off diagonally away from it towards some thicker cover, in which he would be able to hide should he need arise.

It was as well that he did so, for he had not gone very far when what he feared came to pass. Two blacks, carrying spears, suddenly pushed their way out from the bamboos and looked about them in a manner that would have been unnecessary had their purpose been innocent. Keeping close to the swamp, and bending low, they began to move towards the spot from which the smoke had arisen. Ginger had of course dropped flat the moment they appeared. Peering between the grasses he watched them with concern, if not consternation. So the bandits were about, after all, he thought anxiously. To carry out Biggles's instructions was obviously going to be a matter of some danger.

The two natives, to his alarm, now began to cast about as if looking for tracks. Then, rounding some bushes, they saw the fire which, although Ginger had stamped it out, was still smouldering. Crouching, spears ready for instant use, they advanced towards it. What happened after that Ginger did not know, for some trees coming between them, hiding them from view, gave him an opportunity to remove himself from a locality that had become one to be avoided. Moving quickly but carefully in order to leave no track he hastened into the nearest cover, and still keeping a watchful eye on the bamboos, carried on towards his objective.

It was a nervous, uncomfortable walk. He could see nothing, hear nothing, to account for it, but he could not shake off a feeling that he was not alone, that something was likely to happen at any moment; and his nerves became taut as a result. He stopped often to peer ahead, to listen, and to look behind him. In particular he feared that the natives he had seen might be expert enough to follow his footsteps, although he had put his feet down with the greatest care. He wondered where the men were, and what they were doing. He almost wished that he could see them. A peril that can be seen is often less disturbing than one that is suspected, but remains unseen. However, he made progress, and in rather more than an hour had covered what he judged to be about three miles, without encountering anything more dangerous than a warthog.

He should now, he estimated, be opposite the place to which Biggles had referred. He had no proof of this. The bamboos were too tall, and he was too close to see over them. All he could see was the edge of the green bamboo belt. For a moment he considered checking his position by climbing some distance up the hill behind him; but he soon abandoned the idea because it would take time, and he did not want to keep Biggles waiting longer than was absolutely necessary. The alternative was to climb a tree, although he was not sure that this would give him enough elevation.

Deciding that it would not take long to put the matter to the test he chose a tree, parked his equipment at the foot of it, and went up. From the top a glance told him all he needed to know. He was at the right place. The bamboo swamp was a mere three hundred yards or so across, with a fringe of brown elephant-grass on the far side. This was not all he saw. Out in the open, sitting on a knoll beyond the elephant-grass was Bertie, evidently waiting for him to appear.

In his delight Ginger nearly let out a hail; but the recollection of the two natives checked him, which as events turned out was a fortunate thing.

Descending the tree with some haste he picked up his gear and started blithely on the last lap of his journey, confident that his troubles were at an end. Whether or not the secret road continued on through this narrow part of the swamp he did not know, although he imagined that it did. But now that he was within sight of home, so to speak, he did not give the matter serious consideration.

In the light of what happened he felt that he should have done; felt that he should have acted on the assumption that the two natives he had seen were not alone. Their furtive manner made it almost certain that they were members of the Elephant's gang, in which case it was unlikely that they would be far from the main body. However, at the time, in his haste to get back to Biggles, he gave no thought to this, but plunged into the tangle of vegetation determined to put it behind him in the shortest possible space of time.

The going, he found, was not easy. For one thing the ground was softer than he expected. At one point, the lowest part of the swamp, he found himself in sheer bog in which he sank to the knees, with the result that he got very hot and angry. But presently the ground began to rise a little, so that there was some drainage, and the going became firmer. He stopped to mop his streaming face before making his final effort.

He was about to move on when, from somewhere ahead of him, there came a sound that caused him to freeze in his tracks from shock, so unexpected was it. It was a human voice, pitched in a sort of husky whisper. For a moment, wondering if he had heard aright, he stood motionless, heart palpitating, listening for a repetition of the sound. None came, but he thought he detected a rustle as if something, or someone, was moving. This threw him into a state of indecision. He did not feel like going back. Nor, for that matter, did he feel like going on. But as he could not remain where he was he decided that the only thing to do was find out what was ahead of him, if this could be done without taking any outrageous risks. Very slowly, therefore, and taking infinite pains not to make a sound, he went forward, parting the bamboos gently with his hands and peering ahead before taking each step.

In a few minutes his worst fears were realised. Just in front of him the bamboos thinned, and there, crossing his path, running lengthways down the swamp, was the secret road. But it was no longer deserted. It was animated with black bodies, at least a score of them, a few carrying rifles but the majority armed with spears. They were moving about quickly and silently under the hand signals of an enormous African who, in ostrich-feather head-dress and leopard-skin kaross, could only be the Elephant himself. Ginger could not see his face. His back was towards him, as was the case with most of the men, who were being lined out on the far side of the track. At that moment Ginger could have shot the man quite easily, and he was to wish later that he had done so.

It did not take him long to work out what was happening. Cetezulu knew what he himself knew; that Bertie was sitting just beyond the fringe of the swamp. Taken by surprise, he would be an easy victim. The others were no doubt there, too, equally unprepared for an attack. The Mosquito could not be far away. Cetezulu, moving with his gang along the track, had probably seen it land. Indeed, had he been within a mile he could hardly have failed to do so. It must have been Cetezulu who, seeing the smoke, had sent two men to investigate. So thought Ginger.

These thoughts went through his head in a flash, throwing him into a state of agitation that can easily be imagined. It was obvious that he would have to do something, and quickly. What could he do? His first idea was to fire a warning shot and then run. But that, he realised, would be sheer suicide. The Elephant's men would be on

65

him before he could get clear of the swamp. He would have no chance at all. He might shoot one or two but the end was inevitable.

His next plan, he thought, was a better one. It would convey the necessary warning to Bertie, yet give him an opportunity to conceal himself until the others took a hand, as he was sure they would. In a moment he had turned about and was retracing his steps at a speed which, a short while before, he would have thought impossible. His great fear now was that the Elephant would launch his attack before he could sound the alarm.

Panting with excitement and exertion Ginger got clear of the swamp and raced for the tree from which he had made his reconnaissance. Dropping everything except the rifle, which he slung on his shoulder, he went up the tree in a way that would have done credit to a monkey. Reaching a convenient crutch he threw a leg over it and looked out. His relief was great when he saw that Bertie was still there, in the same position. He was obviously unaware of what was going on within a hundred yards of him. For the rest, nothing had changed.

Unslinging his rifle Ginger pushed a cartridge into the breech, took quick aim at a spot a few yards to Bertie's right, and pulled the trigger. The shock had the desired result. Indeed, it nearly defeated its object, for it kicked up a spurt of dust much nearer to Bertie than Ginger intended, striking the ground within a yard of him. However, it succeeded in its purpose, and the speed with which Bertie moved would in different circumstances have brought a smile to Ginger's face.

Snatching up the rifle that had lain beside him, Bertie sprang to his feet, and holding the weapon ready for use backed quickly behind the knoll. Other movements caught Ginger's eye. Algy came into sight, running, some distance farther along the swamp. Biggles sprang into view from a group of trees some way back. Looking hard, Ginger could just make out the Mosquito parked in the shade of them.

He hoped, and expected, that this would be the end

of the affair. Cetezulu, he thought, seeing that his surprise attack had failed, would withdraw. This did not happen. The thing may have gone too far. Possibly some of the Elephant's men took the shot to be the signal for attack. At all events, from the far edge of the swamp where they must have been waiting burst a ragged line of natives. Yelling, they charged up the slope of the knoll that Bertie had chosen for a look-out. Shots cracked. A native pitched headlong. The others ran on. Ginger was appalled by the speed of all this, for it began to look as if Biggles might be overwhelmed after all. Bertie and Algy were both retiring on the aircraft, but the pursuit was swift, and Ginger did not see how the Mosquito could be started up and get clear before it was attacked.

What followed held him tense with surprise as well as anxiety. Clearly, it was the result of some quick thinking on Biggles's part. Ginger could hear him shouting, although to what purpose he did not know. Apparently the others understood. Biggles sprang into the cockpit of the machine. Bertie and Algy, perhaps fifty yards ahead of the nearest native, ran straight to the tail unit, put their shoulders under it, and lifted. This of course brought the Mosquito into flying position with its fuselage parallel with the ground. Another instant and its four Browning machine guns were streaming flame as they swept the ground in front with a hail of lead. The effect of this was instantaneous, and not surprising. Most of the natives turned and fled back to the swamp—those that were able to. A few swerved to one side, either to get out of the line of fire or to force home their attack from the flanks; but Bertie slewed the machine round to cover the threatened direction and a short burst was sufficient to cause them to change their minds. That was really the end business as far as the actual fighting was concerned. It was also nearly the end of Ginger.

He had his rifle snuggled into his shoulder hoping to catch sight of the Elephant, and so he did not notice that the Mosquito had been swung back to cover the swamp. Either by accident or design, Algy and Bertie dropped the tail just as Biggles fired a final burst. The bullets, sweeping low over the tops of the bamboos, sprayed the area beyond, some of them slashing chips from the branches of the very tree in which Ginger was ensconced. Dropping his rifle, he went down the tree even faster than he had climbed it, and made haste to get behind the trunk. And there he squatted, weak from reaction, while silence settled over the scene.

Presently he heard the Mosquito start up and take off, to fly up and down, sometimes over the swamp and sometimes beyond it, as if Biggles were trying to locate the blacks. He thought he heard gun shots above the roar of the motors, but he was not sure. As he expected, Biggles failed to find anything, and after a little while he heard the machine go down in its original position.

Controlling his impatience, Ginger sat still for about half an hour to give the situation a chance to settle; or, to be more precise, to give Cetezulu and his gang a chance to remove themselves from the locality. After what had happened he did not think the Elephant would try any more charging tactics; nor would he linger within range of machine guns. Ginger kept close watch on his side on the swamp, but seeing no movement of any sort he rose at last to his feet, and with some trepidation, rifle at the ready, set about the passage of the bamboos.

With what care he approached the secret road can be imagined. But there was nobody on it, so he crossed quickly, and pressing on, emerged from the elephant-grass just in time to prevent Biggles and Bertie from entering it a little lower down, to look—as they presently explained—for his dead body.

"Are you all right?" was Biggles anxious greeting.

"Right as rain," answered Ginger.

"D'you know what's happened here,"

Ginger looked pained. "Do I know? Have a heart! I started it."

"You started it!"

"Too true I did."

"Why?"

"Because there seemed to be a fair chance of Bertie being turned into a pin-cushion."

"How did you start it?"

"By rattling the pebbles near Bertie's elbow with a bullet."

"Did *you* do that?" cried Bertie, in a shocked voice.

"I did," confessed Ginger. "I tried to warn you."

"I'd have you know, my lad," said Bertie seriously "you thundering nearly hit me."

"I aimed about ten yards to the right of you."

"Then the sooner you put in some target practice, the healthier it will be for the rest of us. Yes, by Jingo," declared Bertie "you made me drop my eyeglass. Luckily it fell on the grass."

"If I hadn't popped off that shot you wouldn't be needing one by now," Ginger told him indignantly. "If that's all the thanks I get for——"

"All right, stop talking rot," broke in Biggles. He looked at Ginger. "Was the Elephant in that bunch?"

"He was."

"Did you see him?"

"I think so. At any rate there was a big negro all dolled up with feathers, lions' tails and leopard-skins. It must have been the Elephant."

"Smart guy," sneered Bertie. "He was too smart to charge with his pals. He sat back while they did the dirty work."

"Where were you all this time?" demanded Biggles, still addressing Ginger.

"Up a tree."

"Doing what?"

"With the place crawling with cannibals, what d'you suppose I was doing—making daisy-chains?"

Biggles smiled. "Okay. You look about all in. Let's get back to the machine and talk about it."

"What about the casualties?" enquired Ginger, looking round.

"The enemy took them with him, to save leaving evidence lying about, I imagine," answered Biggles. "He's welcome to them. It saves us a lot of trouble. The Elephant is the man I want. By the way, did you see which way they went? I know they disappeared into the swamp, but I didn't see a movement afterwards. I could see no sign of them from the air."

"I'll tell you why you couldn't see them when I've had a drink and found somewhere to sit," promised Ginger. "I don't mind telling you that what with storms, gorillas, savages and what have you, I've had enough to go on with."

"What you really need, old boy, is a bath," murmured Bertie sadly. "You may not have noticed it, but you positively stink."

"You should be glad I'm here for you to notice it," returned Ginger grimly. "But for me, you wouldn't be able to smell anything by this time. If you don't like my aroma, go and carry on with your sun-bathing."

They reached the trees. Algy was there, Biggles produced a flask of coffee. Ginger threw himself on the ground and drank deeply. "That's better!" he sighed.

"Now tell us about it," requested Biggles. "You can take your time. There's no great hurry. Algy, keep an eye on those bamboos, in case the Elephant decides to have another go at us."

Sitting in the shade, Ginger narrated all that had happened to him since he put Mishu down at Latonga.

"Jolly good show, old boy!" murmured Bertie, when he concluded. "No joke bumping into a gorilla, no, by Jove!"

"What's the next move?" Ginger asked Biggles.

"It's a pity about the Auster," murmured Biggles, "but there, these things will happen. I don't see that we can do anything about it. All we can do is go back to Kampala."

"Why Kampala?" Ginger looked surprised.

"What else can we do?"

"How about keeping the Elephant on the trot?"

"Where?"

"In the bulrushes."

Biggles shook his head. "Waste of time. What you may not realise is, that bamboo belt stretches for close on two hundred miles. In places it's over ten miles wide. We're only on the southern end of it here. We might rattle it with lead for a month without hitting anything. No. Our best chance is to watch the other end. The Elephant is still heading north. He's bound to come out somewhere. When he does we'll be waiting. But we'll talk more about that when we get home. Let's go."

CHAPTER 8

DEATH INTERVENES

FOR the next few days patrols were maintained over the zone north of where Cetezulu and his followers had disappeared. In particular, watch was kept on the end of the bamboo belt; but it was all without result. The Black Elephant might have sunk into the swamp for all the signs there were of him. Yet, as Biggles remarked, there was nothing surprising about this. Indeed, it was only to be expected, for not only was there unlimited cover, but the Elephant was merely employing the tactics in which, from long practice, he had become expert; tactics which had enabled him for so long to defy retribution. For even in Africa the law has a long arm.

Ginger flew up to Latonga to see if Mishu had any news. But the Masai was not there, and had left no word of his whereabouts. Ginger waited all day but did not see him. Simmonds appeared to have departed. At all events, he was not at the Rest House.

Biggles spent a good deal of time studying the map, marking off the estimated day's march of the Elephant, if he were still heading northwards. This, of course, could give only the roughest possible idea of Cetezulu's position, but it was the only method available. Biggles reckoned that the gang, if it had carried on at its usual speed, must have reached Lake Albert, which forms the boundary between Northern Uganda and the Belgian Congo. On the Belgian side, the country between the lake and the Blue Mountains was such that air reconnaissance was really a waste of time. The Elephant, Biggles opined, was in it; in which case nothing could be done until he broke cover at the north end, where the Albert Nile, which rises at the lake, flows into the Anglo-Egyptian Sudan. He said he was considering moving the base to Juba, in order to be nearer the suspected area, which would save a certain amount of flying time.

At this juncture an event occurred which, while not directly affecting the operation, threw the whole party into a state of gloom, which smouldered into anger, and had the effect of an added incentive to maintain the hunt to the bitter end no matter how long it might take. As Algy put it, it made the matter a personal one.

What happened was this.

Bertie and Algy had just come in from a dawn patrol in the Mosquito—they had been looking for the enemy's cooking-fires—and they were all standing on the airfield talking the matter over, when there appeared from the north an aircraft which was quickly identified as a Puss Moth of pre-war design. It landed and took on some fuel. All this was so commonplace that nobody paid much attention; but presently, when the occupant—the pilot was flying solo—came walking briskly towards them, they paid more attention, thinking it might be someone they knew. It turned out to be a stranger, a young man of about twenty, keen-eyed, alert, and the very picture of health. He introduced himself as Bruce Allan of Edinburgh. He was a member of the University Air Squadron.

"The airport manager suggested that I came over and had a word with you," he began. "He said you'd been here for some time and thought there was just a chance that you might be able to help me."

"How can we do that?" enquired Biggles.

"Well." The Scot smiled a trifle sheepishly. "It may

sound silly to you but I've lost my father. I'm looking for him. He is Dr. Allan, of the Horticultural College, the well-known botanist."

"Go ahead," invited Biggles, smiling. "I haven't noticed any odd fathers knocking about. Where did you lose yours?"

"It's like this," explained Allan. "About six months ago my father decided to make a trip to Mount Ruwenzori to look for some rare plants that are known to exist there. He told me he would not be away for more than four months. In any case, he promised to be back for my twenty-first birthday, which occurred seven weeks ago. My father is a man who keeps his word, and when he didn't turn up I began to get worried. I gave it another week and then asked the authorities in London to make enquiries. I got their report a fortnight ago. It wasn't very satisfactory, although I realised there was little they could do; and, after all, it isn't their affair. All they know is, my father, with plenty of native porters, started off for Ruwenzori, sometimes known as the Mountain of the Moon. Half-way up the mountain the porters packed up. They said they couldn't stand the cold and refused to go any farther. Not having much in the way of clothes that was fair enough, if that was how they felt about it. They turned back and my father went on alone."

"How do you know that?"

"Some of the porters, who returned to their village, have been interviewed. They made no bones about it. My father paid them off. He was in good health when they last saw him, preparing to go on to the top. I'm pretty sure now that something must have happened to him. He may have fallen sick, or had an accident. Anyway, I decided to go and look for him. I couldn't just sit at home doing nothing. So I bought an old Puss Moth and came out. I understand that Ruwenzori covers an area of sixty-five miles by thirty, so there didn't seem much point in wandering about on foot."

"We've done quite a bit of flying over the lower slopes of Ruwenzori," answered Biggles. "We didn't go over the

73

top, of course, having no reason to. But we've made several flights round the lower part. We haven't seen anything looking like a white man."

"I made a crash landing at six thousand feet and had to walk down," put in Ginger, with a wan smile."

"Oh well. Thanks very much. If you do see anything you might let me know. I shall be about."

"Watch the weather," advised Biggles. "The rainy season may break at any time. We've had one storm."

"I'll be careful," promised the pilot cheerfully.

"Come over at about four and have a cup of tea with us?" invited Biggles.

"Thanks a lot," acknowledged Allan. "I'll be along. I'll go and give my machine a look over, although I had no trouble on the way out. See you later." He went off.

"We might ask him to keep an eye open for the Elephant, while he's cruising around," suggested Algy, as they strolled to the bungalow.

"I'll tell him to keep clear, if he does see him, too," stated Biggles.

Curiously, perhaps, it did not occur to any of them that Allan would make a reconnaissance the same day. They assumed, perhaps, that after his long run out from England he would have at least one day's rest before pressing on with his quest. It was with some surprise, therefore, that, shortly after lunch, they heard the Puss Moth take off, and going to the door saw the machine heading west.

"He's not wasting any time," observed Algy.

Biggles frowned. "Had I thought he was likely to do a show today I'd have warned him to keep plenty of altitude," he said. "I've already had a bullet through a wing."

"Not much chance of anyone doing any damage with a single shot," put in Ginger, casually.

"That odd chance sometimes comes off," returned Biggles seriously. "I don't believe in taking unnecessary risks, however remote. I remember, years ago, when Sir Alan Cobham was flying down the Tigris, a single bullet from an Arab on the ground killed Elliot, his navigator, stone dead. The machine was flying at four thousand feet at the time, speaking from memory. Micky Mannock, the top ace of the first war, was also killed by a single bullet from the ground. So it can happen."

Nothing more was said on the subject.

Lunch over, Biggles and Ginger went out in the Proctor to reconnoitre the country between Lakes Edward and Albert. In the air, Biggles averred, there was always a possibility of picking up a clue. They would learn nothing at the airfield. However, they failed to find anything, and a little after four they returned for tea.

As they taxied in, Ginger remarked that he couldn't see the Puss Moth.

"Probably put it under cover for the night," surmised Biggles.

But when they got to the bungalow and were informed by Algy and Bertie that the Moth had not returned, Biggles looked concerned. "Unless it's on the ground somewhere it must be getting short of petrol," he said.

"Allan was to be here at four o'clock for tea," reminded Algy. "I should have thought he'd be here by now."

"We'll give him a bit longer," said Biggles.

Half an hour passed. Biggles got up. "That lad's on the carpet somewhere," he declared. "We'd better go and look for him. Algy, take Bertie with you in the Mosquito and cover the ground south of Ruwenzori—the sides of the mountain, I mean. I'll take Ginger in the Proctor and work to the north. Keep in touch and let me know if you see him."

The two machines took off, but soon parted company, the Mosquito bearing southward and the Proctor edging north. Biggles flew the Proctor, watching the sky, while Ginger made a methodical search of the ground. They failed to find what they were looking for. Biggles quartered the ground for an hour, and then, with the sun nearly down to the horizon, turned for home. "Tell Algy to pack up," he said. "It'll be dark presently."

Ginger continued to watch the ground, and his perseverance was rewarded. "There he is!" he cried.

"Where?"

Ginger pointed to where the Puss Moth stood, on even keel, well out on the open plain some distance to the north of their line of flight on the outward journey. The reflection of the setting sun on the wing revealed its position, otherwise it might easily have been missed.

"Give Algy the okay," ordered Biggles. "Tell him to go straight home."

He stood towards the grounded machine, losing height, and was soon circling over it. There was no sign of the pilot anywhere.

"He managed to get down," observed Biggles. "I can't see anything wrong. Must have had engine trouble. Don't tell me the silly fellow is trying to walk home."

"I can't think he'd do that," returned Ginger. "He'd know we, or someone, would come out to look for him when he didn't show up."

"True enough," agreed Biggles, continuing to circle. "Funny business. Where could he have gone? From the direction his nose is pointing he was on his way home when he went down." Presently Biggles continued, in a different tone of voice. "Is it my imagination or does that look like someone sitting in the cockpit? Watch." With his wheels skimming the ground he cruised past the Puss Moth's nose.

"Yes—it does—look like somebody," said Ginger, conscious suddenly of a dryness in the mouth.

"I'm going down," said Biggles briefly.

He put the Proctor on the ground and taxied on to the Moth. There was still no movement. They both jumped down, and without speaking hurried forward. Biggles opened the cabin door and stood rigid. Ginger, too, stopped. Neither spoke.

Allan was sitting in his seat. His safety belt was still fastened. But one glance at the waxen face told Ginger the worst. "He's dead," he breathed.

Biggles did not answer. His eyes roved the cockpit. He stepped back and looked quickly round the landscape.

"Snake-bite," suggested Ginger, in a whisper.

"No. He wouldn't be sitting like that if a snake had bitten him."

Biggles's face was pale and grim as he returned to the cockpit. Reaching forward, he touched something on the ground. The hand that he withdrew, and showed to Ginger, was red. He investigated further. "Bullet. Came up at an angle through the bottom of the fuselage," he announced, in a brittle voice.

"The Elephant! "

"Wouldn't be anybody else."

"We should have warned him."

"No use talking about that now. We weren't to know what he was going to do. What brutal luck! He must have been cruising very low over the bamboos. Naturally, after what has happened, the Elephant would think it was us. He'd shoot at any machine in range. A thousand to one chance came off, and it was Allan's bad luck to stop one."

"It didn't pull him down right away."

"No. He turned for home. This is as far as he got. Queer how a fellow, mortally wounded, will so often last long enough to get his wheels on the ground—and make a good landing, at that. I've seen it done more than once."

Ginger shook his head. He couldn't trust himself to speak. He felt stunned. It seemed impossible that Allan, so full of life so short a while before, was dead.

"We'll get him home," said Biggles quietly. "You go on in the Proctor and tell them I'm coming. I'll fly the Puss. There doesn't seem to be anything wrong with it but I'd better have a look round."

They found a bullet-hole in the wing, and another in the tail plane, but neither was likely to affect the machine.

"My guess, for what it is worth, is this," said Biggles. "He was flying low, and saw something—some of the Elephant's men in the open perhaps. He went right down for a close look and the whole bunch let drive at him. He wouldn't be expecting anything like that, of course. Well, it's another notch on the Elephant's tally. We'll cut a notch or two, I hope, before we finish. All right. Get cracking. I'll handle this. Tell the Station Manager what's on the way and ask him to have an ambulance standing by."

"Right," said Ginger, and turned away, feeling that in him a new resolve had been born. He couldn't bring the dead man back to life; but he could, and hoped fervently that he would, make the murderer pay.

It was twilight when he landed. Algy and Bertie were waiting.

"What's happened?" asked Algy quickly, looking at Ginger's face.

"Allan's had it," answered Ginger simply. "Shot from the ground. Biggles is bringing him in, in the Puss."

Algy stared. "Dead! Shot from the ground? That means—the Elephant——?"

"Biggles thinks so. Let's go and tell the Station Manager."

                    ⁘ ⁘ ⁘ ⁘ ⁘ ⁘ ⁘

Bruce Allan was buried the next day, the funeral being attended by everyone on the airfield. Biggles made a statement to the police, which was corroborated by Ginger. The Puss Moth was put in a hangar to await instructions about its disposal. There the matter ended, officially. But there was no laughing in the bungalow that evening.

It may be said here that the mystery of Dr. Allan, F.R.H.S. was never solved. He never returned to civilisation, and a search party sent out later failed to discover a single clue. So Africa added two more to its long line of tragedies.

CHAPTER 9

WHEELS WITHIN WHEELS

IT was a grim and subdued party that assembled on the day following the funeral of the young pilot who, in seeking his father, had lost his own life. Nerves were on edge, with the result that little was said until, breakfast over, Biggles produced a map and opened it on the table.

"What's that?" asked Ginger.

"What does it look like?"

"A map."

"Good. As a matter of fact it's Bruce Allan's map," explained Biggles. "I found it on the floor of his machine. I thought it was of no use to anyone except us so I kept it."

"You think it might help us in this Elephant business?" enquired Algy.

"It might. Allan was apparently a methodical chap and had given his job some thought. He must have decided that it was no use blundering about any how, so he divided the area into sections, each one numbered. I imagined he intended to do one section a day. See what I mean?" Biggles pointed at the map and the others leaned forward to look.

Radiating from Kampala, six lines had been drawn in the direction of the Ruwenzori *massif*. They were numbered one to six, and in each case the compass bearing had been noted.

"It's reasonable to suppose that he would start with number one," went on Biggles. "In fact, I'm pretty sure he did. It's borne out by the position of the Puss, where he put it down on the way home. What I mean is, he must have been hit while he was flying along the line marked number one, probably where it crosses the bamboo belt. That tells us where the Elephant was at that particular time. It doesn't mean that he's there now, of course. He would keep moving; but knowing roughly the speed he travels we can reckon that he is now between sixty and eighty miles north of the line marked one on the map. We can't rely on that, though, for this reason. When we first contacted him he was well to the rear of the stolen cattle. But he was catching up with them. Witness the fact that Ginger heard a cow moo, and found the skin of a calf. By this time, I think, he must have caught up with the herd, and the whole gang, and the cattle, are moving together. In that case, naturally, progress would not be so fast as when the Elephant was travelling without any encumbrances."

"Okay," said Ginger eagerly. "We know pretty well where the ruffian is. What are we going to do about it? That's what I want to know."

"And that's what *I* want to know," returned Biggles. "What *can* we do, while he's in those infernal bamboos?"

"The trouble is, we don't know how far the secret track goes," put in Algy.

"I'd say that track goes on to the northern limit of the bamboos, and that's another hundred miles," returned Biggles.

"But it would be a fantastic job, making a track that length," argued Algy.

"Not at all. Bamboo, this thin sort, isn't hard. A score of men walking in line would work through it nearly as fast as they could walk. I can see now that it was this track that made the Elephant's long distance raids possible. Obviously, he wouldn't get far if he had to stay in the open."

"Couldn't we set fire to the beastly stuff and burn the rascals out?" suggested Bertie.

"It wouldn't burn," Ginger told him. "It's too green and lush, and wet in the bottom."

"Why not tackle the track on foot, and chase him out of it?" said Algy.

"Have a heart," protested Biggles. "I don't mind taking chances provided they're reasonable, but to tackle

that bunch in thick cover would be asking for trou[ble]
We're not tackling one man, or even two or three. Th[e]
gang is pretty big, now. We know that because we've seen
some of them."

"How about cutting in somewhere ahead of his line of
march and making an open area where we could see him,"
suggested Ginger.

"That would mean transporting labour to the place,"
Biggles pointed out. "While we were doing that he'd be
well on his way."

"Let's get some bombs, and lay a stick or two along
the track," offered Bertie. "That'd give the blighters
something to think about, yes, by Jove."

"And blow a lot of helpless cattle to pieces at the same
time," expostulated Biggles.

"Botheration!" exclaimed Bertie. "My ideas are never
any use. What about doing a sort of commando raid by
night? We might catch the Elephant alive. If we could
bump him off the gang would fall to pieces."

Biggles shook his head. "I can't say that the idea of
prowling about in those overgrown bulrushes, in the dark,
appeals to me."

"Then what's the use of finding him if we can't do
anything about it?" cried Ginger. "Does it mean that we
can't do anything until he comes out of the green
stuff?"

"I'm afraid so," said Biggles evenly. "That hidden track
is the snag. How could we have anticipated such a thing?
But we do at least know it's there."

"And a lot of use that is to us," grumbled Algy.

Biggles frowned. "All right—all right. It's no use letting
it get us all hot and bothered. There's no future in that.
We'll think of something presently."

"All the time that black devil is at large he's liable to
go on killing people," said Algy, morosely.

"D'you suppose I don't realise that?" answered Biggles,
in an exasperated voice.

"What about consulting old Mishu?" suggested Ginger.
"He should be an expert at this sort of game."

"That's the first sensible suggestion that's been made," declared Biggles. "Let's run up to Latonga to hear what he has to say about it."

"I couldn't find him the last time I went," reminded Ginger.

"He may be back by now," replied Biggles. "We needn't take both machines. The Mosquito will do. I suppose everyone wants to come?"

"I'm bored stiff drooling about here," muttered Algy.

"Same as you, old boy, absolutely," agreed Bertie.

"All right. Then we might as well get along," said Biggles. "Put some food on board, one of you. It isn't likely that we shall be back for lunch. Put a couple of rifles in, too, in case they're needed. You never know what you're going to run into in Africa."

The blazing orb of the sun was nearly overhead when the Mosquito touched its wheels on the baked earth of the Latonga airstrip. Not a soul was in sight.

"Mishu isn't here, or he'd be out to meet us," remarked Biggles, as he taxied right up to the rest-house.

They got out, went into the Government building, and surveyed the ground around it, but to no purpose. "Not a sign," said Biggles. "Moreover, it looks as if he hadn't been here for a day or two," he went on in a puzzled voice. "What can have happened to him? I'm afraid something must have happened or he wouldn't stay away, knowing that we were likely to look him up. There's no message—nothing. Very odd."

"I wonder if they know anything about him in the village?" said Ginger. "There's a native kraal somewhere. I haven't seen it, but it's over there somewhere, in that dip —about a mile, according to Simmonds." He pointed.

"If anyone knows, they should," agreed Biggles. "Come to think of it, one would have thought that some of the men of the village would have come along to look at us, or to sell us chickens or eggs or something. Most natives have seen aircraft these days, but they're generally happy to stand and look at one on the ground. Let's walk along. No one's likely to touch the machine."

They found the kraal without difficulty, an evil-smelling group of bee-hive-shaped grass huts in a depression, at the bottom of which was a pool of stagnant water. A few head of cattle grazed near it, or stood dejectedly in the shade of an occasional clump of trees. Apart from a small patch of corn, trampled flat, no attempt had been made at cultivation. A few men and women lolled about, but most of them slipped furtively into the huts on the appearance of the white men. Some children that had been playing also disappeared.

Biggles called to the half-dozen or so men who remained. They came slowly, and, it seemed, unwillingly, with expressions that were anything but friendly. Biggles asked who was the headman. One, older than the rest, was pointed out, which was an admission that they knew some English, as was to be expected near an official rest-house where white visitors were not uncommon.

Biggles announced the object of his visit. Had anyone seen Mishu, whom they must know? The answer was a sullen silence. Biggles repeated the question with some asperity, whereupon the headman said he knew of no such man. This was a palpable lie, for Mishu had said he was well known there; and before his disappearance he must have been often in the village for food and water. Biggles tried bribes. They failed. He tried threats, to make the natives speak. But he did not persist for long, for it was apparent that the men were going to stick to their story. If they had decided to close their lips, nothing would make them open them.

Biggles turned away. "Come on!" he told the others.

As soon as they were out of earshot, he continued. "Those louts are lying. They know plenty, and for that reason they're going to say nothing. They've been up to something, although whether it is anything to do with Mishu we don't know, and we're not likely to find out by asking them. I'm very much afraid, though that something has happened to Mishu, or the people of the village would not behave like that."

"Something to do with poaching perhaps?" suggested

Ginger. "We're on the edge of the Bungoro Reserve. Naturally, they wouldn't like Mishu, knowing he was gun-bearer to Major Harvey, a game warden. Simmonds told me that poaching was going on in the district."

"Maybe that's the answer," murmured Biggles. "There's another possibility," he continued, as they walked on towards the rest-house. "You may have noticed that these people have some cattle, in spite of the fact that they're close to what we think is the Elephant's line of march. Why hasn't the Elephant taken them? The answer may be that they know all about him and his movements, and they keep their mouths shut as a *quid pro quo* for being allowed to keep their cattle."

They went on to the rest-house. Biggles said little during a picnic lunch, but when it was over he announced the decisions he had reached. "The more I think about it, the more sure I am that something has happened to Mishu, and the people in that village know jolly well what it is. Obviously, we can't just go back to Kampala and leave it at that. Mishu is working for us, and I'm going to find him, or find out what has become of him. Our proper course, no doubt, would be to report the matter to the Government. But anything with red tape attached to it can only move slowly, and meantime, anything could happen to Mishu. I'm going to stay here and watch what goes on. Ginger, you can stay with me. Algy, take Bertie with you back to Kampala. In the morning you can bring both machines up here. We may be here for a time, and need them. Bring some cans of food with you. We've enough to last till you get back. I'm reckoning that when the people in the village see the machine go they'll think we're all in it. If so, they may make a move that will tell us something. We'll keep under cover here and watch. Of course, there's always a chance that Mishu will show up. If so, well and good, he'll find us here. But a feeling is growing on me that he won't. That nasty lot in the village may look dumb, but I'd bet they're listening all ears for the machine to take off."

They continued talking about the mystery of Mishu's

disappearance for some time. Then Algy and Bertie went out to the Mosquito, which was soon on its way south. Biggles and Ginger remained in the rest-house, watching, thinking that some of the men from the village might appear. But they saw nothing of them. The landscape remained deserted, the grass shining in the heat of the late afternoon. The day wore on. Twilight settled over the wilderness. In a solemn hush, as if every living thing was watching, the sun sank into the horizon and night dropped its dark cloak over the scene. But Mishu did not come. In the direction of the kraal there was no sound. Not a light showed.

"I'd like to know what's going on in that village," said Biggles after a time, speaking in a low voice as if reluctant to break the silence. If ever I saw a fellow look guilty it was that headman."

"Is there any reason why we shouldn't have a look round?" said Ginger.

"None. But it would be better to wait for the moon so that we can see what we're doing."

"They're not likely to try anything on with us, I suppose?"

"No. They may be a bad lot, but I fancy they've got more sense than to interfere with white men. They may not know we're here."

Nothing more was said. Ginger nibbled a biscuit, sitting just inside the open door, staring into the gloom.

As soon as the moon announced its approach by a silver radiance that dimmed the stars, Biggles made a move. He picked up a rifle, loaded it and put on the safety catch. "The thing is to be absolutely quiet," he said. "If you must speak, come close and whisper. Sounds travel a long way on a night like this."

"Shall I bring the other rifle?"

"Please yourself."

"I think I will. It gives me a comfortable feeling. Besides, I've just remembered something."

"What is it?"

"Wasn't there some talk about a man-eating leopard in these parts?"

"Yes, now you mention it, there was. The Air Commodore mentioned it in connection with Major Harvey. I think Raymond said a missionary made a vague report about somebody being mauled by a leopard. It was one of the reasons why Harvey came here. If I remember rightly, he didn't find it. But there, the thing may have been merely a rumour. Even if it wasn't it's no unusual thing for someone to be killed by a wild animal. Mishu said nothing about it. Anyway, I don't think we need worry about that."

Walking slowly, and stopping often to listen and look about them, they made their way to the village. There was not a light, not a movement anywhere. Biggles beckoned Ginger nearer and they both sat in the inky shadow of some shrubs to watch.

"I should have thought that with a man-eater about they'd have kept some fires burning," breathed Ginger.

Biggles nodded. "The beast may have been killed, or moved somewhere else."

Time passed. Not a sound broke the heavy attentive silence that hung over the place. The only thing that moved was the moon, which climbed higher into the heavens throwing shadows in hard relief.

"I don't think there's anything doing here. We might as well go back," said Biggles at last.

Hardly had the words left his lips when from one of the huts nearest to them came a rustle. Several figures emerged. There was a low whisper of conversation. A torch suddenly broke into a crackle of flame, revealing clearly the hut, the figures of the men, and in particular the one who held the torch—if it was a man. At first Ginger was by no means sure. It appeared to be a bundle of rags and feathers, but it moved, so he decided that it must be a man.

In the bright orange glare of the torch a barbaric picture took shape. It consisted of perhaps a dozen men, armed with spears, who raised a long burden on their

86

shoulders and then moved forward, following the man who held the light aloft and sometimes waved it from side to side. This leader, Ginger realised, was the local witch doctor; but what mysterious rites were being performed he could not guess.

The procession, increasing its speed, went through the village, out the other side, on a little way, and then disappeared over the lip of the depression. That it did not go very far was made evident by the glow of the torch, and the brief interval of time before the party returned. The men now walked upright, in a tight group. They no longer carried a burden. Reaching the pool of stagnant water the witch doctor dipped his torch in it, extinguishing it with a hiss. The party then broke up, the figures hurrying to several huts into which they disappeared. All movement ceased. Silence returned.

When it became clear that the performance was over, Ginger turned enquiring eyes to Biggles's face. "What d'you make of that?" he breathed.

Biggles shook his head. "Those fellows dumped something outside the village."

"Could you see what it was?"

"No."

"Any idea?"

"Not a clue. But I'm going to find out. It may explain a lot." Biggles rose to his feet. "Come on!" he said softly. "Not a sound."

It took them a little while to reach the far side of the village, for Biggles did not follow the way taken by the natives, which passed between the huts. They made a detour round the rim of the depression until they reached what they judged to be the spot where the torch had halted.

At first there appeared to be nothing there except what looked like, and was, in fact, the stump of a tree, surrounded at varying distances by shrubs and an occasional tree. But the most outstanding thing was an overpowering stench. Ginger grimaced. "Phew! What a stink!" he muttered.

Biggles did not answer. He had stopped, and was staring at something that lay at the foot of the stump. Ginger stared, too, and fear dried his lips when he thought he detected a slight movement. "What is it?" he asked, in a strained voice.

Biggles ignored the question. With his rifle held forward ready for instant use he went on, a step at a time, to the stump. Reaching the object that lay there he bent down, peering. Then, suddenly, with a sharp intake of breath, he put his rifle on the ground and took out his knife.

Ginger joined him. "What is it?"

"Mishu."

"Mishu!"

"Yes. Gagged and trussed up."

"What's the idea?"

"Food for the hyenas, what else?" Biggles was already sawing at the thongs that bound the helpless man. "Use your nose," he said curtly. "The place stinks of carrion. Keep your eyes skinned. I don't think those natives will come back, but there may be something else about." Still working on Mishu, Biggles pulled the gag clear and threw it aside; and Ginger was overjoyed to hear the Masai gasp something. He had feared he was dead. Mishu soon showed that he was not by sitting up and helping Biggles with his task.

Satisfied that the Masai had come to no great harm, Ginger turned to obey Biggles's order about keeping watch, and at once went cold all over when he found his eyes held by another pair, eyes that seemed to glow with internal fire as they caught and reflected the light of the moon. They were low down, on the edge of the nearest scrub, some twenty yards away.

"Look out!" he warned, shrilly.

Biggles snatched up his rifle and whirled round, to see at once what Ginger could see. "Don't shoot unless it comes for us!" he snapped. "It's a tricky light."

How long they stood there Ginger did not know. Mishu shook off the last of his bonds, and picking up a spear, joined them. Then, suddenly, without a sound, the twin lights went out. Biggles did not move. "Will he come, Mishu?" he asked.

"If he is hungry," said the Masai calmly. Even as he spoke, what looked like a black shadow came streaking over the ground towards them. So close to the ground was it, and so silent, that Ginger would have taken it for a shadow, had such a phenomenon been possible.

Biggles's rifle crashed. With a terrifying roar a lithe body shot high into the air. It fell, snarling horribly; but it came on, although not so fast. Biggles fired again, Ginger firing at the same time. Again the animal roared and swerved aside into some bushes, where it could be heard crashing about. Biggles fired three more shots in the direction of the sound. After that there was silence.

"Did we get him, do you think?" asked Ginger anxiously, still holding his rifle at the ready.

"I don't know. I don't think he'll come again anyhow."

"What was it?"

"A lioness, I fancy."

"Leopard," said Mishu, still watching the bushes into which the beast had disappeared.

"If that brute is only wounded he's liable to kill somebody," remarked Ginger.

"The people he's most likely to kill are those in the village, and they deserve all they get," replied Biggles coldly. "Why should we take any chances by following the beast into cover, for their benefit. A wounded leopard should keep them in their huts, and that suits us. Let's get out of this. Mishu, are you able to walk?"

"Yes, *bwana*."

"You're not wounded?"

"No, *bwana*."

"How did these rascals capture you?"

Mishu said they had put poison in his food, and when he was helpless, tied him up.

"You can tell us all about it presently," said Biggles. "We'll get to the rest-house before these rogues come out to see what the shooting was about."

Mishu declared that they would not dare to come out, knowing that the shots must have been fired by white men.

"All the same, we'll get along," decided Biggles. "I don't like the smell of this place."

As they walked on Mishu explained that it was the place where old men and women, who were no longer any use, were put. Also, he added darkly, people who the headman or the witch doctor did not like. In that way it was always easy to account for a death. Tomorrow they would have taken the thongs from what was left of his body. They would show the white men the remains, saying, "This was Mishu. Here is his spear, which was lying beside him. He was killed and eaten by a lion."

"And we would have believed it," admitted Biggles.

"Now *bwana* will understand why there are man-eaters," said Mishu naïvely, as they reached the rest-house.

"But why did they do this to you?" asked Biggles.

"That, *bwana*, is what I shall tell you," answered Mishu.

Ginger lit a candle and prepared to make tea on a primus stove. Biggles examined Mishu's wrists and ankles. They were chafed, but not seriously.

Presently a cup of tea and some biscuits were put into the Masai's hands.

"Now tell us all about it," invited Biggles.

CHAPTER 10

FOOTPRINTS TELL A TALE

SQUATTING on the floor of the rest-house, in the uncertain light of the candle, Mishu told his story. And it was an even more sinister one than Ginger expected. It took some time to tell, but, briefly, the essence of it was this.

90

A white man had been murdered. Some natives, members of the Bungoro Tribe, had seen hyenas digging. Investigating, they found the body of a white man who had been hastily buried. In panic, they re-covered the body and fled. They said nothing about this for fear the blame should fall on them. No doubt they hoped that the body would never be discovered, for if it was, somebody would have to be hanged. He, Mishu, had heard of this, and had gone to the place to find out if the story was true. It was, and the man who had been killed was *bwana* Simmonds, the game ranger who had been to Latonga on government business. He had been killed by a bullet in the head.

To say that Ginger was shocked would be to put it mildly. He assumed, incorrectly, as it turned out, that this was more of the Elephant's work.

Mishu continued. Simmonds's rifle—indeed, all his equipment—had vanished. It had no doubt been taken by the murderers. Mishu had found a cartridge case, but it was not the sort used by Simmonds, so it might fit the rifle used by the man who had shot him. Mishu had covered the grave with stones so that it could not again be disturbed by hyenas.

The Masai, with all the native love of the dramatic, kept the vital part of the story until the end. There were many tracks, he said. Some, of course, were made by the Bungoro who had found the body. But there were others. Some were made by men who did not live in that part of the country. Two tracks were made by men who wore leather boots, such as white men wear. One set of these tracks had, of course, been made by Simmonds. The other was larger, and had been made by a man who was heavy.

Mishu narrated how he had followed the tracks made by Simmonds to some bushes, not far from the grave. Simmonds, he thought, had approached the place through these bushes, and had stood in them, watching something, for a long time. Hanging in the bushes Mishu had found a curious thing. So saying, he got up, went to a corner

91

of the room, and with the point of his spear, started digging up the earth floor. Scraping away the loose soil he produced, wrapped in a piece of cloth, an empty cartridge and a camera, in a case. He held up the camera. "This is what I found hanging in the bushes," he announced. "The murderers had not known it was there."

"That was Simmonds's camera," said Ginger. "I saw it when I was up here."

"Go on, Mishu," requested Biggles.

The Masai seated himself and resumed. That was all he had discovered at the scene of the murder. He had returned to the rest-house, and finding no one there, had hidden the things he had found. He had then behaved rather foolishly, he thought. He had gone to the village and told the headman of the murder, saying that there would be big trouble. He did this because he was well known there, and he thought it would prepare them for the enquiries that would certainly be made. What he should have remembered, admitted Mishu ruefully, was that there had been poaching in the Game Reserve, and doubtless the people in the village knew more about it than they pretended, even if they were not the actual poachers—which he now believed they were. And it was for this reason, to shield themselves when the enquiries were made, that they had done what they had. They thought, perhaps, it would be better if the body of Simmonds was never discovered. They would then pretend ignorance of what had happened to him. But he, Mishu, would tell his master, so they resolved to kill him in a way that would look like the work of a man-eater.

Without any suspicion of this, Mishu had accepted a drink of native beer, which must have had something put in it, for he remembered nothing for a long time; and when he woke up, he was tied hand and foot with rawhide thongs. That night he was carried out to be eaten by the leopard that lived near the place of death. That was all. By what magic he had been found, and rescued, was beyond his understanding.

"We searched for you," Biggles told him. "When you

could not be found we went to the village and asked questions. No one would answer, which made us suspicious, so we kept watch. There was no magic in it. Tell us, Mishu, where did this murder take place?"

"To the north," answered Mishu, "close to the frontier of the Sudan."

Biggles looked at Ginger. "That puts the Elephant in the clear. He couldn't have got as far as that in the time."

Mishu agreed. He was sure Cetezulu was not in the district or he would have heard of it. He thought it more likely that the murder was the work of poachers, who had been caught by Simmonds in the act.

"But according to the tracks there was another white man in the affair," Biggles pointed out.

Mishu admitted that he could not understand that. Sometimes bad white men came from the north to buy ivory, which the poachers dared not take to Kampala, Nairobi, or any other town. His late master, Major Harvey, had told him of this. He thought it unlikely, though, that such men would kill another white man.

"But that's obviously what must have happened," declared Biggles. "You say Simmonds was killed with a bullet, not with spears."

Mishu pointed out that some natives carried rifles, given to them by the traders from the north to enable them to shoot elephant, rhino and antelope.

"What was Simmonds doing with the camera?" put in Ginger. "Why leave it in the bushes?"

Biggles shrugged. "He may have been trying to get some good pictures of big game. Or he may have hoped to get shots of dead animals to prove that poaching was going on."

"That's more like it," declared Ginger. "Simmonds told me about the poaching. His trouble was, he could get no co-operation from the natives, which made it look as if they were concerned in it. It was almost impossible to get evidence. My guess is he brought that camera along in the hope of getting pictures which might secure a conviction."

Biggles looked at Mishu. "You say *bwana* Simmonds's tracks came from the bushes. From which direction did the other tracks come, and which way did they go?"

"They came from the east," answered Mishu. "And they went to the south-west. I followed them, but lost them on some stony ground."

Biggles examined the camera. "There's a roll of film in this." He looked at the number shown in the red disc. "Seven have been exposed. They may tell us something. As soon as we've got a machine here someone can slip down to Kampala and get them developed. There's nothing more we can do for the moment, so we might as well see about getting some sleep. I'll take first watch, just in case anyone comes along and tries to make trouble."

Ginger did not argue. He lay down and was soon asleep; and he did not move until Biggles woke him up just before dawn to take his turn. As soon as the sun appeared he made tea, put out what food remained, and called the others to breakfast. Mishu, he noted, seemed no worse for his ghastly experience.

They had only just finished when the Mosquito arrived and Algy joined the party. The machine was followed shortly afterwards by the Proctor, which Bertie had flown up. Biggles told them what had happened in their absence, whereupon Algy offered to go back to Kampala in the Mosquito to get the films developed.

"Get back as quickly as you can," requested Biggles. "While we're waiting for you, we'll go and have a look at the scene of the murder." He turned to Mishu. "How far away is this place?"

"A day's march, *bwana*."

"Then it won't take us long to get there in a plane," said Biggles. "Is there any place near where we can land?"

"Yes, *bwana*, the ground is all flat, although there are some bushes and a few trees. But beware of anthills."

"All right, let's try it," said Biggles.

Algy, taking the camera, was soon in the air. The others

got into the Proctor which, under Mishu's guidance, was not long reaching the scene of the crime.

There was, after all, little to be seen except a pathetic heap of stones that to Ginger served to make the place all the more lonely. Mishu pointed out the bushes in which he had found the camera. "That is the way the killer went," said he, pointing with his assegai towards the south-west. "From there he came." He pointed a little to the north of east.

"How many were in the party?" asked Biggles.

Mishu said he thought there was one white man with four or five porters.

Biggles considered the route in conjunction with his map. "They must have come from the region of Lake Rudolf," he said slowly. "Beyond the northern tip of the lake is Ethiopia. I wonder . . ."

"Much trouble comes from that place, *bwana*," said Mishu. "Many bad white mens come looking for gold and buy elephant tusks from black men in Uganda and Kenya. They hide because it is against the Government."

"I wonder if we could spot this hound who shot poor Simmonds," surmised Biggles, considering the landscape reflectively. "He can't have got very far."

"He won't be expecting trouble from the air," remarked Ginger.

"That's true—yes, by Jove!" murmured Bertie.

"Of course, this isn't really our affair," went on Biggles. "Our job is to find Cetezulu. But it goes against the grain to let this unknown thug get away with murder. Still, before we start anything we'd better go back to Latonga and see if Algy has found any of interest in those photographs."

They returned to the airstrip. Algy came in soon afterwards, and he brought with him information that exceeded in importance anything for which they could have hoped. This took the form of some photographs, still damp, between sheets of blotting-paper. These made it clear at a glance that the unfortunate game ranger had secured the evidence he sought. Seven films had been exposed, and all had given clear, sharp prints that spoke well of Simmonds's ability as an amateur photographer.

The first two prints were of the same subject, and showed a number of natives hacking the tusks out of a dead elephant. The two photographs had been taken from the same spot, but the position of those in the pictures had altered somewhat, so that between the two, most of the faces could be seen. Ginger recognised one of them instantly; and so, from their exclamations, did Biggles and Mishu. It was the headman of the village.

"No wonder he didn't want to talk," said Biggles grimly.

The next two prints showed simply the remains of a dead rhino, with its horns cut off. Vultures were feeding on it, but no human beings were there. The beast looked as if it had been dead for some time.

The last three prints were so dramatic, and so startling in what they portrayed, that a hush fell on those who looked at them.

"By Jove! What d'you know about that!" murmured Bertie at last. "Talk about every picture tells a story."

"These certainly tell one, and it's an ugly one," said Biggles quietly.

"They were the last three films exposed," put in Algy. "I reckon they must have been taken just before Simmonds was shot."

"That's about it," agreed Biggles. "I'd say he got his photos, put the camera in the case and hung it up out of the way—which rather looks as if he was expecting trouble. Either he was spotted, or with more nerve than sense, tried to make an arrest."

These photographs were all of the same subject. They showed a heavily-built white man, dressed, or even over-dressed, for where he was and what he was doing. He wore crossed bandoliers. Field-glasses hung round his neck. A belt round his waist carried a heavy hunting-knife. A conspicuous feature of his face was a dark, rough beard. Two natives, carrying spears, dressed in ragged, ill-fitting shirts and trousers, stood on either side of him. Their faces were unlike those of the local people, several of whom were in the picture, standing expectantly, facing the white man. Between them lay some articles that left no doubt as to what was going on. They were four elephant tusks, two of them very small, and several rhinoceros horns. These, obviously, were about to change hands. The picture showed the bargain being struck.

Biggles drew a deep breath. "Well, poor Simmonds certainly got something, though it cost him his life. Nothing could be more conclusive than this. He must have tracked those natives to their rendezvous with the rascal who buys the stuff. I wonder who he is? Do you know this man, Mishu? Have you ever seen him?"

Mishu answered that he had never seen the man, but he had heard of him and knew him by description. The man, he said, was not altogether white. He came from Ethiopia, where he had lived for some time. There was a story that the man had once been rich, but had run away from his own country in Europe to live in Addis Ababa. Mishu thought the man had first come south into British territory looking for gold, but not finding any had started a traffic in illegal ivory, leopard-skins, and anything the people had to sell. He had had this information from Major Harvey, who had sometimes looked for the man but had never been able to find him.

"If he gets back across the frontier, there will be nothing we can do about it," said Biggles anxiously. "If we followed him there someone would set up a howl about violating other people's territory. However, if we move fast we may be able to head him off before he can get back. If Mishu's reading of the tracks is correct he hasn't started for home yet. I'll make a cast towards Lake Rudolf in the Mosquito, for a start, to see if he does happen to be heading that way. Algy, you take Bertie with you in the Proctor and try your luck in the other direction. Grab plenty of altitude so that if the man sees you he won't suspect you're looking for him. For the same reason, if you spot him, carry straight on before you turn. On no account fly low over him. Keep in touch. I'll take

D

Ginger and Mishu with me."

"Fair enough," agreed Algy.

In a few minutes both machines were in the air, heading for their respective beats.

Biggles reached the north-eastern territory at two thousand feet. He then throttled back to cruising speed and began a methodical search of the ground. For some time the only remark he made was to the effect that he thought they must be over the boundary between Uganda and the Sudan, although there was of course nothing to indicate it, the terrain on both sides being similar. The machine was now following the course almost due east, and looking at the map, Ginger observed that they must be within a hundred miles of Ethiopia.

Presently Biggles indicated a glittering streak of light that filled the horizon directly in front of them. "Lake Rudolf," he said.

Ginger turned his eyes back to the ground, paying some attention to an extended mark that had puzzled him for some time. It was not distinct enough to be a road, yet it was much too wide to be a game track. Sometimes it faded out, only to appear again farther on, always running eastwards in the direction of the lake. He noticed that it appeared to link up the occasional water holes. He asked Mishu what he thought it was, assuming that he had been over the ground. Mishu replied that it was a long time since he was there. He could not remember seeing it. It might be a cattle-track, although it would need many cattle to make such a mark on the hard ground.

"Surely that would depend on how often the cattle used it?" said Ginger.

"You may have got something there," stated Biggles. "The thing I can't understand is, there isn't a sign of life of any sort. I haven't seen a single head of game. In country as thinly populated as this one would expect to see plenty of antelope and wildebeest."

Here Mishu interrupted to say that if Cetezulu came that way there would not be many animals. He would need much meat to feed all his men. Apart from that, animals soon leave a district where they are shot at constantly.

This remark, made casually, presented to Ginger a possibility that had not occurred to him. "Look here!" he said in a voice of enlightenment "could there be any connection between the Elephant and the man we're looking for, I mean, could they all be part of the same gang?"

"I was just turning that over in my mind," answered Biggles. "It wouldn't surprise me. We've already decided that Cetezulu must hand over his looted cattle to somebody. According to Mishu, this fellow who killed Simmonds comes from Ethiopia. May be that's where the cattle go. The fellow with the beard might well do a bit of game poaching as a side line. But what's that I see ahead? Is it smoke?"

"It is smoke, *bwana*," confirmed Mishu. "There is a camp—big camp. Many men."

"How very interesting," murmured Biggles. "We may be getting somewhere."

Ginger, peering ahead, saw that the strange mark that had been under discussion seemed finally to disappear into the vast area of jungle, swamp and river, that occurs where the frontiers of Uganda, Sudan, Kenya and Ethiopia, meet, near the northern tip of Lake Rudolf. On the near side of this several fires were smouldering. A number of natives were moving about, but on the approach of the aircraft they stopped what they were doing and looked up.

"Have we struck the Elephant's hide-out?" questioned Ginger eagerly.

"I don't see any cattle," said Biggles.

"No white man there," put in Mishu. "If white man there he look up and we see white face."

"What sort of men are these, Mishu?" asked Biggles, flying straight on.

Mishu declared that from their dress they were men from Ethiopia. They had no business there. They had no right to cross the frontier. Only bad men would do that.

"This business is beginning to hook up," asserted Biggles. "That track could only have been made by cattle. What cattle? Obviously, the stolen cattle. There's no other explanation. This looks to me like the terminus of Cetezulu's long trail, the place where he sells his loot and then goes into hiding. All these Ethiopians now over the frontier must be part of the same racket. They wouldn't come here on their own account. They've got a leader, and there's not much doubt about who it is."

"You mean the man who buys the poached ivory—the swine who killed Simmonds?"

"That's the answer," returned Biggles. "My guess is, the gang we can see below are the drovers waiting to take the cattle into Ethiopia."

By this time the Mosquito, after making a wide circle, was flying back over its course.

"If the cattle ever get as far as this, we should never stop them," remarked Ginger presently.

"I'm not particularly interested in the cattle," replied Biggles. "I want the men; Cetezulu, and this pale-faced murderer who, unless I'm off my bearings, has a date with him. I——"

"Wait a minute! Hold it!" interposed Ginger sharply. "Here's Algy." He listened for a minute or two, his eyes on Biggles's face.

"They've spotted him!" he announced.

"Who?"

"The poacher. Just a minute! Go ahead, Algy. Yes . . . I've got it. Okay."

"Tell him to go straight back to Latonga," ordered Biggles. "We'll do the same."

Ginger passed on the order. "Okay, Algy—see you presently. We're on our way. So long."

"Good work," said Biggles, satisfaction in his voice. "Where did Algy spot him?"

Ginger answered. "He says the man has four natives with him. They've made camp beside a stream about twenty-five miles south-west of Latonga, between the northern limit of the bamboo swamp and a big belt of elephant grass. They've got a tent pitched."

"Fine! We should be able to pick him up," said Biggles, pushing the throttle wide open.

"If the aircraft doesn't make him take fright and bolt into the swamp."

"I don't see why it should. He must suppose he's quite safe or he wouldn't be where he is. In the ordinary way it might take weeks for news of a murder to reach the Government. Game wardens are sometimes away for months at a stretch, so it wouldn't be thought odd if Simmonds didn't report to his headquarters for some time yet."

"You intend to grab this fellow, then?"

"I'm certainly going to try."

"What about the Elephant?"

"With a bit of luck we'll get him too. Why do you suppose that fellow, with a murder on his hands, is hanging about? Why doesn't he get across the frontier while the going's good? Judging from the photographs he's collected the native ivory. What's he waiting for?"

"The Elephant."

"That's my guess," agreed Biggles. "More than the Elephant, he wants the stolen cattle. I don't suppose he pays the Elephant the full price for his herd. In Ethiopia a big herd would be worth a fortune. Once this fellow gets the cattle he won't sit around very long. That's why I'm going to have a crack at him now, instead of handing over the job to the police. And I'll tell you something else. The Black Elephant isn't far away. He must be about due. That's why I'm hoping to get both these red-handed scoundrels in the bag at the same time."

"This white man isn't likely to submit to arrest," opined Ginger.

"He can please himself about that," retorted Biggles grimly. "If he prefers to fight—well, that's okay by me. It may save the hangman a job."

He raced on towards Latonga.

CHAPTER 11

A SOLDIER TAKES A HAND

At Latonga a surprise awaited them. Two light trucks were parked outside the rest-house. About them a number of Askaris, soldiers of the African Rifles, were busy at various jobs. Algy and Bertie, who had evidently just arrived in the Proctor, were talking to a white officer who was presently introduced as Lieutenant Haynes.

"Haynes has come down from Juba to investigate a report that a white man has been murdered in this district," said Algy. "I was just telling him that it's true, and that the man was Simmonds of the Game Department. We've been out looking for the murderer."

Haynes looked distressed.

"You knew Simmonds, I gather?" queried Biggles.

"Yes. I knew him well. Nice chap. I was afraid something like this would happen."

"Why?"

"Because he had his own ideas about his job, some of them rather unorthodox."

"Such as carrying a camera?"

"Exactly. And going out without a gun-bearer, or a proper safari. He had a notion that all natives gossip—which of course they do—and so word got around of what he was doing, which defeated his object. So some time ago he started travelling light, alone."

"I wondered why he had no porters?" murmured Ginger.

"It was dangerous," went on Haynes. "Mind you, I wasn't thinking of murder. What I was afraid of was that he'd get hurt taking on a wounded beast. He was quite fearless."

"Why did he come here from Juba? Juba is in the Sudan. This is Uganda."

"I know. But between ourselves it isn't possible to observe the frontiers too closely. It's often necessary to cross from one side to the other, otherwise poachers would just dodge about and laugh at us. But tell me. Have you got a clue of any sort? I was just going to the village to make enquiries."

"You wouldn't have got far," Biggles told the officer seriously. "They're all mixed up in it."

Haynes frowned.

"Don't worry," went on Biggles. "We know who killed Simmonds, and we know where the man is. He isn't a native. He's white—or nearly white."

Haynes looked astonished.

"Actually, we were looking for this black devil Cetezulu, when we struck this," resumed Biggles. "Now you're here, you'd better take over. How did you hear about this business anyway, if you were at Juba?"

"We were told by Kampala."

Biggles looked at Algy. "Did you say anything to anybody when you went to Kampala to get those photos developed?"

"Yes. I had a word with the Station Manager. I didn't know there was any secret about it."

"No, I suppose not," agreed Biggles.

"I started right away and kept moving," said Haynes.

"You didn't waste any time," conceded Biggles. "And you've no time to waste now if you want to grab your man before he skips."

"Have you any real evidence that he did the job?"

"As much as you're likely to need to wind up his career," answered Biggles. "The man came from Ethiopia to buy, among other things, poached ivory. Simmonds got a photo of him doing that—I'll show it to you in a minute. I don't know his name. He's got a black beard. There are four natives with him who my man here says are tribesmen from Ethiopia, but there is a big crowd of porters just this side of the frontier who I fancy are waiting for him. I've worked it out that this fellow's real purpose in being here is to buy all the loot the Black Elephant has collected on his raids in the south; but that remains to be seen. I fancy the poaching was a sideline. It's my belief that he's now waiting for the Black Elephant to show up." Biggles went on to narrate all that had happened since they arrived at Latonga. He concluded by showing Haynes the photographs taken by Simmonds.

The officer's eyes opened wide. "Oh!" he breathed. "So that's the gentleman, is it?"

"You know him?" questioned Biggles.

"Oh yes, we know him—or rather, of him," answered Haynes warmly. "We've been looking for him for a long time. He was a German spy, living in Addis Ababa, when the war broke out. What his real nationality is we don't know, but it's unlikely that he's a German. He calls himself Bronnou, which might be anything. He's put out some cock-and-bull story of being a prince. We'll make a prince of him all right, if we can get hold of him."

"Then you'd better get after him."

"How far away from here is his camp?"

Algy answered. "About twenty-five miles."

"Unless you get cracking he may move before you get there," warned Biggles.

"Yes, it'll take me a little while, whether we march or go in the trucks," said Haynes thoughtfully. "These trucks of ours are useful, but they can't move fast across country without risk of busting something."

"Would you like me to fly you over?" suggested Biggles. "One of your trucks could follow on and bring the prisoners back. My man, Mishu, could go with it and show the driver the way. He knows every inch of the country. We could have the place cleaned up by the time the truck gets there."

"That sounds a good idea to me," declared Haynes. "How many men could you take?"

"Four, in the small machine. That should be enough. I'd rather not risk landing the Mosquito on ground I don't know. Anyway, it would be better for one machine to remain in the air and watch what goes on in case Bronnou bolts. The Mosquito could make things uncomfortable for him if he did. The ideal thing would be to catch him off his guard. Actually, he'd be less likely to bolt from an aircraft than if he saw your trucks coming. It wouldn't take him long to guess what you're after."

"I'll leave it to you," said Haynes. "I'm ready when you are."

Biggles made his arrangements, which were simple. He would fly the Proctor, taking with him Haynes, Bertie and Ginger. Algy was to watch events from the air in the Mosquito and keep track of Bronnou should he try to get away. If necessary he could use his guns. Mishu was to go in the truck with ten Askaris under a sergeant. The remaining troops would keep guard over the rest-house and the remaining truck, which was loaded chiefly with stores and spare equipment. It was arranged that the truck carrying the troops should have an hour's start, to enable it to get near the scene of action before the aircraft went down to make the arrests. On no account was it to show itself until the aircraft landed. Mishu said he knew the place where the tent was pitched, when Algy described it to him. It was a well-known camping ground on account of the water supply.

The truck containing the coloured soldiers was soon on its way.

Biggles and his party sat talking for an hour about the business that had brought them together. Haynes said he knew all about the Black Elephant's criminal record. Like all government servants in Central Africa he was always on the look out for him; but he'd heard nothing of him for some time.

At length Biggles looked at his watch. "Time we were moving," he announced.

As they moved towards the aircraft Biggles told Algy not to follow him too closely. Bronnou might have his suspicions aroused if the two machines arrived together, particularly as the Mosquito was a military type.

Ginger made the trip keyed up for what was likely to be a dangerous operation, and one that might have a vital effect on their own assignment to hunt down the self-styled Emperor of Africa. He was right in both cases.

The opening moves of the business occurred in the order in which they were to be expected. Bertie pointed out Bronnou's camp. The tent was still at the same place. Bronnou was sitting outside on a stool, cleaning what looked like—and turned out to be—a rifle. His four men were squatting in the grass nearby, doing nothing in particular. All faces were turned towards the Proctor as it approached, and Ginger noticed that Bronnou stopped what he was doing, to watch. The wheels of the aircraft touched the ground. The machine bounced once or twice and then ran to a standstill perhaps a hundred yards from the tent.

Biggles and Haynes were first out and started walking towards the camp, whereupon all five men got to their feet and stood waiting for the visitors. Ginger and Bertie followed on. As they drew near, while Bronnou made no move, defensive or otherwise, Ginger could sense a stiffness in the atmosphere. Bronnou, with a guilty conscience, must have suspected their business, he thought, but did not want to commit himself to direct action in case he was mistaken.

Ginger would have distrusted the man even if he had known nothing about him. He was big, powerfully built, about fifty, sallow-skinned, low-browed and cold-eyed. His bushy beard gave him a belligerent appearance. In a vague sort of way he reminded Ginger of a bad-tempered bull. Perhaps the rings had something to do with that, he conjectured. A bull usually has a ring in its nose. Bronnou had a ring, a gold ring, in each ear; which proved, Ginger reflected, that whatever his nationality might be he was not a western European.

Haynes was the slim, wiry type, but he soon showed that he was not to be intimidated by Bronnou's apparent toughness. He wasted no time stating his business.

"I'm Lieutenant Haynes of the African Rifles," he announced curtly.

"So you say," sneered Bronnou, in a husky voice with a suspicion of accent in it.

106

"Get packed up," ordered Haynes. "You're coming with me to Headquarters."

"So you say," repeated Bronnou.

"We've some questions we'd like you to answer."

"So you say."

"Quite right, that's what I said," stated Haynes crisply. "Pack up. Or you can leave your stuff here. I don't care which. Either way, you're coming with me."

"Who says so?"

"I say so—and what I say, goes."

"Oh!" Still Bronnou did not move. His eyes made a thoughtful reconnaissance of the men in front of him as if weighing his chances of resistance. "What's all this about, anyway?" he drawled.

"In the first place you've no permit to enter this territory," answered Haynes curtly.

"I can explain that. Anything else?"

"Yes," returned Haynes, slowly. "I'm taking you in for questioning in connection with the death of Mr. Simmonds, of the British Game Department."

"What makes you think I had anything to do with that?"

"Then you knew about it," flashed Haynes. "How?"

Bronnou's eyes narrowed and took a swift glance at the Mosquito which had now arrived over the scene. "I never said that," he growled. "What are you trying to do—frame me? I've never seen Simmonds—never heard of him."

"Then what are you doing with his rifle?" enquired Ginger. "That Rigby Express you're holding belonged to him. I'll swear to it. He showed it to me the other day."

That did it. Bronnou must have realised that bluff was not going to help him, and he moved like lightning. He whirled the rifle, which apparently was not loaded, round his head, flung it at the men in front of him, sprang sideways like a cat, and with a revolver that appeared like magic in his hand, blazed at Haynes. It all happened in an instant. Haynes spun round, clutching at his arm. By this time Biggles had his automatic out and two shots crashed almost together. Ginger felt the whistle of a bullet on his face. Bronnou staggered back, cursing, tripped over a tent rope and fell over backwards.

What happened immediately after that Ginger did not see, for he became involved in other matters. Two of the natives bolted, but one of the others raised his spear and was about to throw it at Biggles when Ginger shot him. The man fell, shouting. His companion dropped his spear and stood still, his eyes showing the whites. Ginger snapped a couple of shots at the running natives, but knowing what to expect they dodged as they ran, and the bullets missed.

He turned back to the tent to find a desperate battle in progress. Biggles, Bertie and Haynes, had thrown themselves on Bronnou and were trying to hold him down. This was no easy matter, for the man, mouthing with rage, fought like a tiger, even though Bertie was kneeling on the hand that held the revolver. Ginger twisted it free, and was promptly knocked over sideways by a flailing leg—whose, he did not know. He pulled himself up by a tent rope and the feel of the rough cord in his hand gave him an idea. Haynes, obviously, was determined to take his man alive, for he had had more than one opportunity of shooting him, or cracking his skull with one of the several weapons that were lying about. For this reason Ginger did not like to resort to extreme measures, although he felt he would be justified, for the outcome of the affair was still in doubt. In spite of the odds against him Bronnou seemed to be possessed of the strength of ten men, and time and time again he flung off those who were trying to hold him.

Ginger whipped out his knife, cut a length of the rope, and quickly tying a slip-knot managed to get the noose over Bronnou's legs, which he pulled together before securing them to a tent-peg. That turned the tide. Ginger produced more rope, and between the lot of them they managed to pinion Bronnou's arms and legs so that presently he lay helpless, cursing them. Breathless, and looking the worse for wear, the others got up. All had been more or less knocked about, but Haynes was the only one actually wounded. Bronnou's bullet had ploughed through his upper arm, fortunately without touching the bone. He made light of it, but Biggles bound it up with a dressing brought from the emergency kit in the Proctor.

The native whom Ginger had shot sat on the ground, moaning, although as it turned out he was not mortally hurt; the bullet having grazed a rib. The second native still stood there, looking thoroughly scared. The other two had vanished.

"I say, what a messy business," muttered Bertie disgustedly, cleaning his eyeglass, which he had just picked up from the ground.

"It could have been worse," said Biggles, gently fingering a lump on his forehead.

Haynes went into the tent. He was there for some minutes. When he came out he brought a number of objects, which included, among other things, a wristwatch and a petrol-lighter. Ginger identified these as Simmonds's property.

"That's all I want to know," said Haynes grimly.

"Any ivory inside?" asked Biggles.

"No. But he wouldn't be likely to haul that about with him. No doubt he's buried it somewhere, intending to pick it up on the way home. But there's something else inside we'll have a look at," said Haynes.

The others watched him go through Bronnou's pockets. This produced a small bunch of keys, which was, apparently, what Haynes was looking for. He then went into the tent again and came out carrying a metal cash box. This he opened, and in silence lifted out a big wad of notes. Turning to Bronnou, and holding up the wad, he said: "This is a lot of money to carry about—where there are no shops. What was it for?"

Bronnou did not reply.

"I think I can answer that question," said Biggles evenly.

"Here comes the truck," put in Ginger.

"Good!" said Biggles. "Wave the okay signal to Algy. He can go home. We'll get along ourselves when we've got our breath back."

However, they waited while the truck came up, and the prisoners were loaded into it. The tent was struck, and with its contents, put on board. The truck then started on its return journey, the Askaris looking disappointed that their services had not been required. Haynes decided to go with it in order to keep an eye on his dangerous prisoner. Mishu stayed, to go back in the Proctor.

"That should be one rogue less in Africa," remarked Biggles, as the truck moved off. "I'll just have a quick draw at a cigarette before we start," he went on, suiting the action to the word. "What a business! If there's one thing I hate, it's brawling; but what else could we do? I suspected that Bronnou would be a tough customer, but I must admit that I wasn't quite prepared for a raging lunatic."

"He and the Elephant would make a good pair," averred Ginger.

Biggles cast a thoughtful eye over the landscape. "Speaking of the Elephant reminds me: it might be worth coming back here tomorrow. I still have a feeling that Bronnou was waiting for him, which means that we must be on his route to the north. There's plenty of water and cover. I don't often bet, but I'd make a small wager that that bundle of money Bronnou was carrying was to pay for the cattle. For what other purpose would he want so much money in a place like this? He wouldn't need anything like that sum to pay for the small quantity of poached ivory he was likely to pick up here. No. He was going to buy the cattle, and if that guess is right it won't be long before the Elephant is here."

Mishu pointed with his spear to the area of tall elephant grass which started some distance farther down the stream. It was between two and three miles long, with an average width of two to three hundred yards. It was, he said, the place where Major Harvey had been killed.

"That supports what I've just said," Biggles told the others. "If the Elephant used that as a halt on one occasion he may do so again. It may be one of his regular stops. There's water here. I think we can be sure of one thing. He hasn't got as far north as this yet, or we should see the marks of the cattle. What do you think, Mishu?"

The Masai was quite definite that the cattle had not passed.

"The ideal thing would be to catch him when he has to cross the open ground between the bamboo swamp and the elephant grass," said Biggles pensively.

"He won't do that in daylight," declared Ginger. "He'll slip across while it's dark."

"Yes, I think you're right," agreed Biggles, glancing at the sun, now hanging low over the horizon. "We shall soon have to make up our minds what we're going to do."

They were walking slowly to the machine when, through the hush that always falls with evening, from far away to the south there came a sound that brought Biggles to a halt, staring in that direction.

"That came from the bamboo belt, or from somewhere close to it," said Ginger.

Biggles looked at Mishu. "Was that a cow?"

"Yes, *bwana*. It was a cow calling her calf."

"A domestic cow, I mean, not a buffalo?"

"It was a tame cow, *bwana*."

"Is there a native village anywhere in that direction?"

"No, *bwana*. It is fly country."

Biggles knew that he meant that the district was afflicted with the tsetse fly, the carrier of sleeping sickness. He hesitated. "If there are no natives, what are cattle doing there? You needn't tell me the answer. It must be the Elephant, getting his herd on the move to keep his appointment with Bronnou."

"He'll be here before morning, old boy," said Bertie.

"What's he going to think when he finds his dirty partner isn't here?"

"The question is, what will he do?" returned Biggles thoughtfully.

"What else can he do but carry on?" put in Ginger. "He won't want to hang about here with a mob of cattle."

"He certainly will not, if those two natives who got away make contact with him and tell him that Bronnou has been arrested," muttered Biggles. "That news, if he gets it, should put him in a flap. Even so, the only thing he can do is push on—unless, of course, he decides to abandon the cattle. I can't see that happening, though, unless he's really hard pressed. Those beasts represent the accumulated profits of months of work."

Again the distant bellow rolled across the lonely landscape. Two or three others joined in.

"That's the cattle, all right," asserted Biggles. "They're on the move. This may be the chance we've been waiting for. I mean, when he breaks clear of the bamboos."

"He won't stop here in the open," said Ginger.

"No. He isn't likely to do that," agreed Biggles. "His whole policy is one of keeping in cover during daylight. The next cover on his route is that elephant grass. That, I'd say, is where he'll spend tomorrow. We know from Mishu that he's used the place before."

"Look here, old boy!" cut in Bertie. "If you take the machine off he'll hear it. If we can hear his cows he'll hear us—if you see what I mean."

"Yes, I see what you mean," answered Biggles slowly. "On the other hand we can't leave it where it is without a risk of him seeing it. He'll have scouts out, you may be sure. If it comes to that, what if he does hear the machine take off? What can he do about it? Nothing. He may be relieved, thinking we've gone away. It's better that he should think that. Anyhow, whether or not he learns what has happened here, being so near the frontier he'll be anxious to push on. But we're doing rather a lot of guessing. We may be barking up the wrong tree. One cow doesn't make a herd. The thing is, before we commit ourselves to anything definite, to make sure that we're on the right track."

"It's no use flying over the bamboos," said Ginger. "You won't see anything."

"I wasn't even contemplating it," replied Biggles. "The only way to find out what we want to know is for someone to stay here and watch."

Mishu stepped forward and said he was willing to stay.

"Someone ought to stay with him," said Biggles.

"I'll stay," offered Ginger and Bertie together.

"All right," agreed Biggles. "You can both stay. I shan't need you. You can take it in turns to get some sleep. I'll fly the machine back. I want to speak to Haynes, anyway, before he goes. It may be a good thing to have him around for a little while. Keep well back and watch in the direction of the bamboos. If the cattle appear, mark where they go. Be careful! You won't be able to light a fire, of course—but you shouldn't need one. As soon as you've got the gen start walking towards Latonga until you come to a place where I can get down. I'll be along soon after dawn."

"Fair enough," confirmed Ginger.

"Right. That seems to be all. I'll get along," said Biggles, climbing into his seat.

The engine came to life, but Biggles did not take off immediately. Opening the throttle only wide enough to cause the machine to move forward, he taxied cautiously towards where the darkening sky was now merging into the purple shadows of the distant scene.

Ginger turned away. "We'd better find somewhere to park ourselves while there's enough light for us to see what we're doing."

After exploring for some time they decided on a mound covered with rough herbage, which, standing a little way back from the stream, gave a good view of the few miles of open ground that lay between the bamboo swamp and the elephant grass. They all agreed that it was the ideal spot.

Before very long they were to wish they had chosen somewhere else.

CHAPTER 12

THE GREAT STAMPEDE

As the last pink afterglow of the dying day faded into the sombre hues of dusk, somewhere far out on the lonely plain a lion roared, an impressive accompaniment that somehow seemed to be in keeping with the scene. Indeed, so commonplace had this sound become that no one commented on it, all ears being strained to catch the first indication that the cattle were getting nearer. But when, presently, the lion roared again, and was answered by another, Mishu turned his head in the direction from which it came and stared steadfastly into the deepening darkness.

Again a lion sent its awful challenge into the night, and the thought occurred to Ginger that the cattle would not like it. In a low voice he made a remark to that effect.

Mishu agreed. He said he thought the lions might be hanging about on the outskirts of the herd, hoping to find a straggler. He added the comforting information that lions do not roar when stalking their prey. More often they roared after they had eaten and were on their way to water.

Ginger looked at the pale, meandering line, that still marked the position of the stream just below them; but he said no more.

Shortly afterwards two lions roared in unison, somewhat nearer, again to be answered by another. Ginger moved uncomfortably and put his rifle across his knees. He would have admitted frankly, hungry or not, he preferred lions at a distance. Mishu made a sign to keep quiet.

Roaring at intervals, the beasts drew nearer. Mishu whispered that he thought they were coming to the stream to drink. He did not think there was any cause for alarm. If the lions were hungry, he repeated, they would not roar. Ginger found small solace in this, as the moon had not yet risen, and the sensation of sitting in the pitch dark, with lions near at hand, was anything but pleasant. He suggested tentatively that if the lions got any nearer they ought to light a fire; but Bertie wouldn't hear of it, pointing out that a fire would certainly defeat the very object for which they were there. Ginger replied grimly that if they were devoured by lions, that would defeat their object with even greater certainty.

He grimaced as a lion, quite close, drew in its breath audibly before shattering the silence with its dreadful voice. Soon afterwards a swishing in the grass made it evident that a troop of lions was passing close on its way to water. Raising his head slightly Ginger could just see the animals, in single file, against the skyline. Mishu put his hand to his lips for silence; and a little while later the lapping of the lions could be heard, just below them, as they quenched their thirst.

There was an interval of some minutes, and Ginger was just beginning to hope that the beasts had gone away, when, after the usual indrawn breath that sounded like a yawn, one of them roared. Another joined in, and another, until they were all roaring together, emitting such a volume of sound that the ground seemed to tremble and the air vibrate. Nothing that Ginger could have imagined would have been anything like it. They all sat perfectly still, Mishu with his head bent forward, hands over his ears.

The mighty chorus ended in a series of throaty grunts. There was an uneasy silence for a little while; then the whole thing started all over again. Towards the end, to Ginger's unspeakable relief, the uproar withdrew somewhat, suggesting that the lions were now going on their way. From time to time they continued to roar, the sound getting more distant until it stopped altogether.

Ginger, who, unconsciously, had been sitting rigid, relaxed. "Phew! " he breathed. "That wasn't funny. Did you ever hear such an infernal din! "

"Worth hearing, all the same, old boy," declared Bertie. "Wouldn't have missed it for anything. Jolly old fellows at a party, aren't they? I've heard people make sillier noises when they've been drinking—yes, by Jove."

Ginger agreed that the sound was majestic, but he wouldn't care if he never heard it again. He wondered if the roaring would affect the Elephant's plans. It seemed unlikely that he would try to move the cattle with such a frightful noise going on.

In this belief he may have been right, for two long hours elapsed before any other sound was heard. Then, when one did come, it sent them shrinking low in the grass. Human voices spoke, and they were not far off. What was said Ginger did not know. If Mishu knew, he did not open his lips. The sound was not repeated. Presently the moon came up to flood the plain with radiance, and a little later there was a shout in the distance. It was followed by others. A cow bellowed. Others did the same.

"This sounds like what we've been waiting for," murmured Bertie.

They did not move from their position. By raising himself up a little Ginger found that he could see the outer edge of the distant bamboos; but the light was deceptive, and for a long while he saw no movement. Mishu said he could make out a big herd of cattle moving slowly towards them, with men on the outside keeping it compact. He must have been right, for presently, sounds, the usual sounds of men and cattle on the move, became audible. They drew nearer, until, after rather more than an hour, the herd, numbering some hundreds of beasts, grazing as it advanced, was opposite, not more than four hundred yards away. It was a long time passing. Eventually it

116

faded into the mysterious distance, in the direction of the elephant grass.

Mishu said he would follow, to see how far the herd was taken before it was again hidden for the hours of daylight. It would be better if the others remained where they were. Their white faces might be seen in the moonlight by sharp-eyed natives. He would return when he had the information, he concluded, and glided away into the night.

Bertie told Ginger that he might as well try to snatch some sleep. He would keep watch, and wake him if anything happened. He himself was not in the least tired.

Ginger needed no second invitation, for now that there was no immediate cause for anxiety he was suddenly drowsy. Stretching himself out on grass that was still warm after the heat of the day, he was soon asleep.

He was awakened, stiff with the chill of the small hours, by the return of Mishu, with the information that the herd was now grazing near the far end of the elephant grass; and as it was nearly dawn it seemed certain that Cetezulu intended to make the sixteen-foot-high grass his next stopping place.

"In that case, we might as well make a move," suggested Ginger. "That is, if Mishu thinks it's safe."

Mishu said he thought all the Black Elephant's men were with the herd, so it would be quite safe for them to go.

"Did you actually see Cetezulu?" asked Ginger.

Mishu answered no, but from the number of men now with the herd he felt sure that the Elephant and all his followers had caught up with the stolen animals, and all were now moving together towards the frontier.

"All right," said Ginger. "Then let's get clear of this place and find somewhere for Biggles to land. We shall have to go some way to make sure that the Elephant doesn't hear the machine."

"Yes, it's time we got cracking," agreed Bertie. "Biggles said he'd be along about dawnish."

They set off, moving as fast as was compatible with

117

caution, and had covered about two miles before a pallid flush in the sky announced that daylight was at hand. They pushed on, moving faster now, until, finding an area free from obstructions, they sat down to wait.

They heard the machine coming soon afterwards, and a handful of dry grass made enough smoke to bring Biggles, in the Proctor, to the spot. The machine landed, and Biggles, who was flying solo, stepped down.

"Everything all right?" queried Ginger.

"Yes. Algy's waiting at Latonga. Had I brought him with me, I couldn't have got you all in. What's the news?"

"The herd went across the open in the dark, as you expected, and is now in the elephant grass," Ginger told him.

"Did you see Cetezulu?"

"No, but Mishu feels sure that the whole gang has now joined up with all the cattle. We saw the herd go past quite close to us. It's a really big mob. Mishu followed it to the high grass."

"That's capital," declared Biggles. "This is what we've been waiting for."

"What will you do?"

"Winkle him out, of course."

"How are you going to do that?" asked Ginger dubiously.

Biggles smiled. "One thing at a time. Get aboard. I want to stop Haynes moving off. He's anxious to push on home with his prisoners, but he promised to wait till I got back to see if I needed his help."

They all got into the machine, and in a few minutes were at the Latonga rest-house. Haynes and Algy were standing there, waiting. There were also, to Ginger's satisfaction, some breakfast.

"Well, what's the latest?" asked Haynes.

"Cetezulu has done what I thought he'd do," answered Biggles. "I couldn't see how he could do anything else. He's got the herd bedded down for the day in that big patch of elephant grass not far from the spot

118

where you picked up Bronnou. "This is the first real chance we've had of getting on terms with him, and we may never get another. If he makes a dash for that jungle country near the frontier, and gets into it, we've had it. He knows we daren't follow him there."

"True enough," agreed Haynes. "What can I do for you?"

"You can lend me as many of your men as you can spare," replied Biggles. "Cetezulu has a gang of at least thirty men with him and that's a biggish handful for my small party. If I wait for police reinforcements the Elephant may slip away before they get here. Your fellows have rifles, and authority to use them. If you'll post them at strategic points round the grass we shall have the Elephant where we want him. The gang can either surrender or fight it out. If they decide to fight, the responsibility will be theirs if there is bloodshed."

"How are these chaps armed?" asked Haynes.

"Mostly with spears. A few have rifles which were no doubt taken from the people they murdered. But they're only a mob of ruffians, and wouldn't have a chance against disciplined troops like yours."

"I'm your man," assented Haynes. "A sergeant and a couple of men can take care of the prisoners until we get back. That means I can bring ten men along."

"That should be plenty."

"What's the drill? I don't like the idea of sending my fellows into thick cover."

"I wasn't thinking of anything like it."

"What are you going to do, then?" enquired Haynes. "Are you going to try to drive them out by shooting up the grass?"

"No. That might only result in wasting a lot of ammunition. Besides, I don't like the idea of plastering a lot of helpless cattle—that's what would happen. I've a better scheme than that. It ought to work." Biggles took Haynes on one side, and using the bonnet of one of the trucks as a rest, made a quick sketch on a page torn from his notebook. He spoke earnestly while he was doing it. A slow smile spread over the officer's face as he listened. When Biggles had finished Haynes simply said okay, and turning away, began making his arrangements.

Biggles returned to the others. "I'm hoping to push the Elephant out of his lair without firing a shot," he announced. "It may not come off, but I fancy it will. Anyhow, we'll give it a chance before resorting to more direct methods. If it works it should save casualties—on our side, anyway."

"How about telling us what you're going to do?" asked Ginger impatiently.

"I'm just coming to that," answered Biggles, smiling faintly. "There's no hurry. The Elephant won't be likely to move in broad daylight. I'm giving Haynes a couple of hours to get his men into position."

"Then what?"

Biggles's smile broadened. "We'll see how several hundred head of cattle behave when two Merlin engines start howling just over their heads. I don't think they'll like that."

Enlightenment dawned in Ginger's eyes. "You mean— you're going to stampede them?"

"That's the idea. With the herd galloping up and down, that elephant grass will be no place to lie down and go to sleep. Actually, I'm hoping to save the cattle. They can be rounded up afterwards. Cetezulu's men can also be rounded up when they come out of the grass in small numbers, as I think they will. Those who prefer it can stay inside and be trampled into the mud by the cows. They can please themselves about that. I'll fly the Mosquito with you, Ginger. Algy, you and Bertie can follow me in the Proctor. Between us we should be able to make a fair amount of noise."

"Here, I say, this is going to be *something*!" declared Bertie enthusiastically. "Swipe the blighter with his own swag, so to speak. Brilliant, old boy, absolutely brilliant!"

Biggles grinned. "Let's have a cup of tea while we're waiting."

"What about Mishu?" asked Ginger. "Take a look at him."

Mishu was squatting on the running board of one of the trucks, thoughtfully sharpening the point of his spear with a piece of stone.

"He'll have to be in the party," said Biggles. "We can't very well leave him behind. He doesn't like flying, so he'd better go in the truck with Haynes."

"From his expression," put in Algy "he's hoping to push that spear into somebody before the day is out."

"I couldn't care less," answered Biggles. "He's got an old score to wipe out, don't forget. His is a personal grudge. Ours isn't. Ginger, tell him to go in the truck with the Askaris."

Ginger complied. Presently when the truck moved off, among the bristling rifles and dark, grinning faces, there was a solitary spear. The face of the owner of it was expressionless.

After that, with nothing more to do, they sat around over a dish of tea and discussed the project until the time allotted to Haynes had expired. Then they went to their respective machines and took off.

As the Mosquito left the ground Ginger was again conscious of a feeling of exhilaration. Whatever the outcome of the affair, he thought, the Elephant, after his long run of successful buccaneering, was no longer having things all his own way. The gang might stand by him while all went well, but they would soon get tired of being harassed from one end of the country to the other by aircraft, particularly if there was no loot to share out.

The belt of elephant grass, roughly oval in shape, which was the objective, came into sight. There was no wind, not even a breeze, so the tall, slender grass was motionless, giving no sign of what was inside it. Ginger made out Haynes's lorry parked in a slight depression, and some Askaris, lying down on both sides of Cetezulu's retreat. He wondered if these dispositions had been made without Cetezulu being aware of them. If he had observed what was going on outside, what did he think of it? Perhaps he was not worried overmuch, feeling confident that the troops would not dare to enter the grass, where their advantage of discipline and superior weapons would be lost. In that case he would reckon on slipping out under cover of darkness, when again the Askaris would be handicapped by not daring to shoot for fear of hitting each other. If that was what the Elephant thought, pondered Ginger, he was due for a shock.

He must by now have heard the aircraft. That wouldn't cause him any great anxiety, either. He must have heard them often during the past week, and decided that he had nothing to fear from them while he remained under cover. At all events, the grass remained motionless, which suggested that the Elephant did not intend taking defensive action. Indeed, so still was the grass that Ginger had an uneasy feeling that the Elephant might have already slipped away.

Biggles cruised on for a distance beyond the southern end of the grass. There he turned, bringing the machine in line with it. "Hold your hat!" he said calmly. Then, opening the engines flat out, he dived.

For a moment Ginger held his breath, thinking they were going straight into the ground. But ten feet above the grass the Mosquito flattened out, and with engines howling raced across it. Looking down Ginger saw the grass bend under the pressure of the air they displaced. Reaching the far end of the run, Biggles swept up in a steep climbing turn, to repeat the performance as soon as the Proctor, which had followed them, was clear.

Actually, it seemed to Ginger that there was no need to do any more. Once had been enough, and even with that the effect must have surpassed even Biggles's most optimistic expectations. At the northern end the tall grass was lashing about as if it had been struck by a cyclone; and it was not the aircraft that were responsible, for they were both clear. Then, from all angles, the cattle began to burst out. With them were men who, from their behaviour, had no other idea than to avoid being trampled to death.

122

Biggles's face showed no emotion as, swinging round, he dived again, nearly brushing the tips of the already agitated grass. Then, as before, he zoomed, turning, to observe the result.

Ginger stared, fascinated, at such a spectacle as he had never seen before and was not likely to see again. There must have been between four and five hundred animals in the herd, and the sight of that number galloping about in panic may have made the number seem even higher. The grass was rapidly being trampled flat, with the result that it became possible in places to see what was going on inside it. Bullocks and cows were streaming away in all directions, but others, apparently not knowing from what they were trying to escape, tore up and down regardless of men who, far from trying to steady the beasts, were dodging about in a desperate effort to keep clear of the bovine storm. Some that had been knocked down were trying to crawl out. Others lay still. The grass belt began to look as if several tanks had been manoeuvring in it.

A flash of colour attracted Ginger's attention, and focusing his eyes on it he made out a figure which, from its flamboyant attire, he knew must be the Elephant himself. But there was no longer anything majestic in his appearance. His ostrich feather head-dress hung down over his back, and it was clear from his behaviour that he had been infected by the general panic. He ran out of the grass a little way, looked up and down, and started to run again, only to be knocked down by a dozen or more animals that came tearing down the side of the broken grass. He was soon on his feet again, however, with his finery still more dishevelled. He was limping badly.

"There's the Elephant!" Ginger shouted in his excitement. "There he goes! Give him a rattle. Don't let him get away."

Biggles tilted the nose of the aircraft towards the fugitive; but he did no more than that, for racing towards Cetezulu from an angle, to cut off his retreat, was another black man, so that it became impossible to shoot at one without a risk of hitting the other.

"It's Mishu!" yelled Ginger. "Look at him. He means business."

"Of course he does," answered Biggles. "That over-dressed lout murdered his master."

"He'll kill him."

"It's about time somebody killed him."

Spellbound, Ginger could only watch.

Cetezulu saw Mishu coming. Ginger expected to see him shoot the Masai. Then he saw that he had no rifle. Presumably he had forgotten to pick it up after being knocked down by the cattle. Mishu, spear in hand, raced on, concerned with nothing but his quarry. The Elephant, limping badly, seeing that he would be overtaken, whirled round and threw something at his pursuer. What it was Ginger could not see; but whatever it was, Mishu dodged it. He ran in close. His arm went back, and jerked forward. Cetezulu stumbled and fell.

At that juncture some steers collided with them and hid them from view. When the animals had passed on both men were flat on the ground.

"I'm afraid poor old Mishu's had it," Ginger told Biggles.

Biggles did not answer. He turned the Mosquito back over the grass—or what was left of it, for most of it had been trampled flat. There was not a single animal left in it, but Ginger could see several of the Elephant's followers, some sitting, some lying still, some crawling.

"I don't think we need stay up here any longer," Biggles told Ginger. "Tell Algy to go down. We'll find somewhere to get down ourselves. We'd better see the end of the business."

"There seems to be an awful mess down there," observed Ginger. "The cattle are scattered far and wide."

Biggles cruised in circles until he found a place where a landing seemed reasonably safe; then he glided in, and got down without mishap. He switched off. They both jumped down, and hurried towards the scene that was still a picture of confusion as the Askaris rounded up their prisoners and mustered them in groups.

The Proctor was able to land nearer to the spot, and the two crews were soon together. Haynes joined them. "You certainly did the trick," he told Biggles. "What a tale I'll have to tell when I get back. The trouble is, no one will believe me. What happened to Cetezulu? We haven't got him. Did you see which way he went?"

"Yes, he's over on the far side," announced Biggles. "He made a bolt for it but he didn't get far. I fancy my man, Mishu, stuck a spear into him. I should have expected something like that because it was here, on this very spot, that the Elephant murdered Harvey of the Game Department. Mishu was his gun-bearer for years. He never said much about it, but judging from the way he behaved just now he must have been nursing his hate, waiting for the chance he got today to square the account. He may have joined my party with that in view, knowing that he would be more likely to catch up with the Elephant that way than if he worked on his own. But let's go over and see what's happened."

"All right," agreed Haynes. "I think my fellows can take care of things on this side. There doesn't seem to be any opposition. You certainly started an earthquake. If I hadn't seen it I wouldn't have believed it."

They walked on through the trampled grass to discover Mishu sitting up beside the prostrate body of his enemy. The Elephant, shorn of his finery, was lying face downwards, with the haft of Mishu's spear protruding from his back. It was clear that all the Masai's pent up hate must have gone into the thrust. But his face was expressionless when Haynes examined the body.

"Dead as mutton," announced the officer.

For perhaps a minute the white men stood silent, surveying a picture which must be as old as Africa itself.

"Mishu shouldn't have done that," said Haynes gravely.

Biggles shrugged. "You can argue that nobody has the right to kill anybody. Personally, I can't see that it makes much difference whether Cetezulu was hanged, shot or speared. He was due to be killed by someone. If you look

125

at the thing objectively, Mishu has saved everyone, including ourselves, a lot of trouble. He had ample justification, anyway, and I fancy the Government will take that view. But the thing's done so there's not much point in talking about it."

Mishu, it turned out, had remained seated for the very good reason that he had a broken leg, the result of being kicked when he and Cetezulu had been knocked down by the stampeding cows. A stretcher was brought from the truck and he was carried across to where the Askaris were remustering.

"I'll fly him down to Kampala," decided Biggles, watching two stretcher-bearers put the broken limb in a temporary splint. "Do you mind if I leave you to clear up this mess?" he asked Haynes. "I've no facilities for dealing with it."

"Don't worry about that," answered the officer. "We can manage. We're equipped for this sort of thing."

"That's fine," replied Biggles. "In that case we'll push along. I'll make out my report on the whole business when I get to Kampala and send you a copy."

"That suits me," agreed Haynes. "So long! Look in at Juba on your way home if you have time."

"I'll bear it in mind," promised Biggles. "Thanks a lot for coming along."

Five minutes later both machines were in the air on their way to Kampala.

．　　．　　．　　．　　．　　．　　．

Little more need be said. With the death of the man who aspired to be The Black Emperor of Africa, and the imprisonment of the surviving members of his gang, the menace that had for so long disturbed the territory expired, and was soon forgotten. Bronnou was tried, sentenced to death and subsequently hanged, for the murder of Simmonds. The story they told was much as Biggles had surmised. Simmonds, catching Bronnou red-handed buying poached ivory, had tried to arrest him, and was instantly shot dead. With

Bronnou removed from the scene the ivory poaching traffic soon faded out for lack of a market. The stolen cattle were rounded up without much difficulty and returned to the stations from which they had been taken.

Mishu was not long in hospital. On his discharge he was offered the job of gun-bearer to Major Harvey's successor, a post that he still enjoys. The authorities did nothing about his taking the law into his own hands, ruling that he had acted in self-defence after the Black Elephant had thrown a knife at him.

By the time all these details were cleared up, Biggles and his friends were back in London, attending to other matters.

CAPTAIN ARMADA

has a whole shipload of exciting books for you

Armadas are chosen by children all over the world. They're designed to fit your pocket, and your pocket money too. They're colourful, gay, and there are hundreds of titles to choose from Armada has something for everyone:

Mystery and adventure series to collect, with favourite characters and authors – like Alfred Hitchcock and The Three Investigators. The Hardy Boys. Young detective Nancy Drew. The intrepid Lone Piners. Biggles. The rascally William – and others.

Hair-raising spinechillers – ghost, monster and science fiction stories. Super craft books. Fascinating quiz and puzzle books. Lots of hilarious fun books. Many famous children's stories. Thrilling pony adventures. Popular school stories – and many more exciting titles which will all look wonderful on your bookshelf.

You can build up your own Armada collection – and new Armadas are published every month, so look out for the latest additions to the Captain's cargo.

If you'd like a complete, up-to-date list of Armada books, send a stamped, self-addressed envelope to:

Armada Books,
14 St James's Place,
London SW1A 1PF